Large Print Too
Toombs, Jane.
A topaz for my lady fair

Also by Jane Toombs
in Large Print:

The Fog Maiden

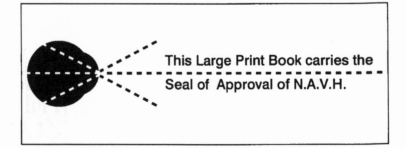

This Large Print Book carries the
Seal of Approval of N.A.V.H.

A Topaz for My Lady Fair

JANE TOOMBS

G.K. Hall & Co. • Thorndike, Maine

Published in 2000 by arrangement with Jane Toombs

G.K. Hall Large Print Paperback Series.

The text of this Large Print edition is unabridged.
Other aspects of the book may vary from the original edition.

Set in 16 pt. Plantin by Minnie B. Raven.

Printed in the United States on permanent paper.

Library of Congress Cataloging-in-Publication Data

Toombs, Jane.
    A topaz for my lady fair / by Jane Toombs.
      p. cm.
    ISBN 0-7838-9042-7 (lg. print : sc : alk. paper)
    1. Amnesia — Patients — Fiction. I. Title.
PS3570.O55 T66 2000
  813′.54—dc21
                                                 00-021094

A Topaz for
My Lady Fair

Risa was suddenly aware of the car. The screech of locked brakes hurt her ears, then the car swerved, its right fender giving her no more than a gentle nudge, but she was off balance and fell sideways into a spiral of nothingness.

The dark silence was infiltrated by whispers of sound, voices, words with no meaning. Risa opened her eyes to sunlight so glaring it sent slivers of pain into her skull.

"My head hurts," she said.

A man knelt beside her holding her wrist.

"I didn't hit her, I know I didn't." A woman's voice. Risa tried to push herself onto one elbow to focus on the speaker but the man's arm held her down. Suddenly panicky, she began to struggle.

"Don't move." The man's voice was low but carried a note of authority. "I want to make sure nothing's broken." Risa felt her arms and legs being moved gently. Then he helped her to sit.

The woman spoke again. "You walked right out in front of my car — I was so scared. But I know I didn't hit you, the fender sort of brushed you is all." A high-pitched voice, unpleasant, a blurred impression of long dark hair framing a thin face.

A wave of nausea gripped Risa and she clutched at her stomach, doubling over. She breathed deeply, mouth open, and the urge to vomit passed.

"Help me up," she said, and as the man's arm tightened about her, leaned into its strength and stood. She wavered a little and her head throbbed.

"I don't see any marks," the woman said. "She isn't hurt."

Risa disliked the whining voice. "I'm all right, I guess." She tried to disengage herself from the man's arm. An urge to hurry from this place caught at her.

"You ought to get her name and address," the man said.

Risa pulled free. "I'm all right," she repeated. She had to get away, away from these irritating strangers. What was she doing here? Risa looked around, not recognizing the tall white building at the end of the parking lot. Had she brought the car?

"Where . . . ?" she began and then decided she mustn't admit to not knowing where she was — she would never get rid of these people. "I'm really fine," she said more positively. "Please don't bother about me." She looked at the man as she spoke. About thirty, tall, brown hair curling to his collar — nothing unusual except the hazel eyes that examined her with concern. Attractive, long-lashed eyes with glints of gold in the iris. Discerning eyes. She turned away.

"Thank you for helping me," she said.

The woman had backed off, edging around to

the driver's side of her car. Risa made a gesture toward her. "She's right, you know. I must have walked out in front of the car. Not her fault. Good-bye — and thanks again."

Risa turned her back and walked slowly away, knowing the man was watching her. Her head pounded with each step but she clenched her teeth and kept going. Hurry from the white building, out of the parking lot! But where was she going? Did she have the car?

I don't even have my purse, she thought. Could I have dropped it when the car hit me? She stopped, turned to look back and saw the man was still standing there though the woman's car was gone.

Risa jerked her head around and kept going. I don't remember, she thought. I don't know if I had a purse or if I walked in front of that car. Disturbed, she thrust her hands into the pockets of her coat. There was something in one pocket. Paper. Risa pulled out an envelope. The flap was only tucked in, not sealed, and she opened it. Money. The envelope was full of money. She counted the bills. Shaken, she leaned against one of the empty cars. What was she, Risa MacArthur, doing in a strange parking lot with no purse and twenty-five twenty-dollar bills in her pocket?

Amnesia? No, no, she knew who she was. But maybe the accident — Didn't people sometimes forget what happened just before an accident? And obviously the woman's car *had* knocked her down. Risa looked at her hands, saw the scraped skin on the palms. And the headache — Had she hit her head?

"I don't think you're all right." The man's voice made her jump. "I'd say you're suffering from mild shock, if nothing else. Quite common after an accident. I wouldn't drive quite yet if I were you."

She stared at his face, saw the concern in the hazel eyes. "Drive?" she echoed.

"Isn't this your car?"

Risa glanced blankly at the blue Mustang she leaned against. "No. I don't — that is, my car's not here."

"My name's Jim Halloway," he said. "I'm a doctor. I really think you should have a more complete examination. I'd like to take you into the hospital emergency room here — or to your own physician if you prefer. Sometimes . . ."

Risa backed away from him, eyes wide. So that's what the white building at the far end of the parking lot was — a hospital. What was she doing here? I've got to get back to Rory, she thought. He'll know what's wrong.

"No," she said. If only she could remember. But her head was fuzzy with pain and her stomach tightened with nausea. She put a shaky hand to her forehead. Her legs were trembling. I'm going to pass out, she thought.

Jim Halloway's arm held her firmly. She felt him push her head down and she opened her mouth to take deep breaths. "Please," she managed to gasp, "just let me go home." Then she began to whirl into the spiraling darkness once again.

Risa's head ached with a fierce, pulsating throb and the sun slanting into her eyes made her wince. She became aware of a sharp aromatic odor in her nostrils as her vision cleared enough to see a man's face above her. A stranger — no, this was the doctor. Why was she lying on the ground, on the grass? She could see the green blades when she moved her eyes.

"Where . . . ?" she began.

"You fainted. I moved you over onto the grass. Now let me go in for a wheelchair and we'll get you into the E.R. and have them take a look at you."

"No, please, not the hospital. I don't want to go in there." Trembling, she tried to sit up.

"Why?"

"I . . ." Panic choked her so words wouldn't come. She couldn't go, didn't he see that, didn't he know? Suddenly she hated him — he was keeping her from Rory, from getting home.

Risa forced herself into a sitting position, fought against the fright and anger blocking her speech. "I want to go home," she said, the words spaced evenly, her voice flat.

There was a silence.

"I'll take a cab," Risa said. She reached for the envelope in her pocket and to her shock found it gone. Had the money really been there? Had she imagined the envelope with five hundred dollars? She stared at Jim Halloway. "You," she said accusingly.

11

His face reddened. "Sorry. I was looking for identification, someone I could call. All I found was . . ." his voice trailed off, and he pulled the envelope from his shirt pocket. "You can count it if you like."

She shook her head and looked away from him.

"I'll take you home," he said. "Let me help you over to my car."

"I live in Del Mar," she said. "How far . . ."

"I'll take you home," he repeated.

Risa sat in the front seat of Jim Halloway's orange Porsche and stared at the green freeway signs. She huddled into her coat. "I'm cold," she said.

Jim glanced at her. "Shock probably. It's pretty warm for November." He paused, then added, "Were you visiting someone at Sharp?"

"Sharp?"

"Sharp Hospital." His voice was impatient.

"No." But had she been? Sharp Hospital, of course! She had seen the building from the freeway often though she had never been there. Until now, she amended. Why had she gone to Sharp Hospital?

"There's a mirror on the back of the sun visor," Jim said.

Did she look that bad? She glanced at her tan car coat and saw the smears of dirt for the first time. Her brown pants were too dark to make the stains on them obvious, but the tear on the right leg was easily seen and her brushed-leather shoes were scuffed and dirty. The coat was familiar, her coat, but she didn't remember buying the shoes. Nor the pants. She had never owned dark brown pants. Risa swallowed, determined not to give way to panic again.

With reluctance, she turned down the visor to look at herself. A little sigh escaped her as she met her brown eyes in the mirror. She realized she had been holding her breath, afraid she might not know her own face. How silly. She did look washed out, skin pale, but her black hair curled familiarly. It was only when she gave her head a toss to throw her hair back from her face that she knew something was wrong. Her hair was not a long dark mass spilling over her shoulders down to her waist. Short curls framed a frightened face.

"What's the matter?"

"My hair — look at my hair." As soon as the words were out she regretted them. Don't tell him, her mind whispered. Better he doesn't know, no one must know. You'll remember. Rory will tell you.

Risa managed a small noise she hoped would pass as a laugh. "I'm a mess," she said. "My hair needs brushing and I think my face is actually dirty. And see my hands." She held her skinned palms out for him to inspect.

"I noticed them," he said. "Beginning to heal. You didn't get those abrasions on your hands in the past few minutes. Not in the hospital parking lot when that car grazed you. Those happened at least several hours ago."

Risa stared at her hands and noticed the scabs

which had formed on the scraped palms. She glanced at Jim and saw he was not looking at her.

"You didn't need to drive me home," she said.

"I feel responsible. Something's wrong. You won't tell me, but I know." He touched her shoulder briefly. "I might be able to help."

"I don't need any help," she said. "I mean not any more than you've given." She heard her voice, clipped and ungracious. Rory's all I need, she told herself.

Jim did not speak again for a time and Risa shrank from the darting minnows of terror that swam in her mind. Who cut my hair? When? Why am I wearing strange clothes? And why can't I remember? I know who I am . . . She turned and looked out the side window to prevent Jim from seeing her face. Can I be sure I'm Risa MacArthur? she wondered.

"Where do I turn off the freeway?" Jim asked, and Risa forced her attention back to the road. Yes, here, the familiar off ramp, then the narrow twisting roads that led to Highway 1 along the shore of the ocean.

"The house is on the bluffs," she said. "We're up high here, the land drops to the water."

"Very nice," he said.

She thrust away his words. They seemed like others she had heard too often: "Expensive, isn't it? Nice to be able to afford the view." You *always* had to pay for privacy, for beauty. What was wrong with that?

Here the road wound first between the pines

on the hillside, then the tall multicrowned euca-
lyptus, their white trunks lining the drive like
naked soldiers.

The house itself was deceptive, only one story
showing from the land side, but it meandered
partway down the cliff in a series of levels. Jim
pulled up by a walkway.

"Thank you," she said hurriedly, hoping to slip
out of the car and escape inside the house before
he could open his door. But he grasped her hand.

"You haven't told me your name," he said.

"Oh — Risa MacArthur."

"Risa. That means laughter." He touched the
side of her face so gently she hardly felt his fingers. "You look so forlorn the name seems
wrong. I wish you'd let me help."

She shook her head, pulled her hand from his.
"Thank you again," she said mindlessly, not
looking at him, wanting only to escape, to find
Rory.

But she stood watching the orange Porsche
pull away from her, saw Jim's wave through the
rear window. She didn't need his help, but when
the car was out of sight she felt deserted, alone
on the walk of crushed shells, harsh under the
rubber soles of her shoes. Her head still hurt.

At last she turned and walked slowly toward
the red door, her steps quickening as she approached. The brass knob was cold under her
hand. Rory's name was on her lips but the impulse to call to him died away as she stepped into
the darkened house. Why were the drapes drawn

across the windows? The sun should be flaming in, lowering now in the west, flooding the house with gold and crimson. Rory hated to have the windows covered.

She crossed the slate of the entry, stepping onto the thick yellow carpet. Where was he? Upper deck lounge? No, the rooms on the first level were deserted. Downstairs, then, in the main living room.

Risa passed from one room to another without finding Rory. Finally she went down the steps to the last level, where the kitchen and laundry rooms were. Here the windows were not draped and the sun brightened the lower deck lounge, picking out the dust on the tables. I'll have to get after Beatrice, she said to herself. She knows better.

The door to the kitchen was closed. She swung it open and saw bowls scattered over the counter tops, preparations for a meal obviously under way. A pot bubbled on the stove but the kitchen was also empty. As she stood looking about, the outside door opened and a girl in a lavender pantsuit came in. Her long blond hair caught the sun and glistened but her blue eyes stared coldly at Risa.

"Who are you?" the girl demanded. "What are you doing in this house?"

Risa stepped back before she caught herself. "Where's Beatrice?" she asked.

"Went to the store," the girl said. She seemed to relax, smiled at Risa. "I didn't realize you knew her."

Risa wanted to say, It's my house, you're the one who doesn't belong. But fright paralyzed her vocal cords. She watched the blonde walk past her to peer into the pot on the stove. My age, Risa thought. Maybe a little older. Twenty-five? Very pretty. But certainly not related to Beatrice. Risa cleared her throat. "Who . . . ?" she began.

There was a noise from the stairway, creakings, the rustle of paper.

"Sounds like Bea now," the girl said.

Risa left the kitchen. She certainly would speak to Beatrice about this stranger in the house, making herself at home. She started toward the stairs, saw the wide body of the housekeeper clump down the last few steps, looked at the round brown face with pleasure and relief.

"Beatrice," she said.

The woman's dark eyes stared at her for a few seconds.

Risa moved forward. "It's Risa," she said, hearing the anxiety in her voice. "I'm home."

"My God," Beatrice said and the bags of groceries she held in her arms slipped from her grasp. "Dear Jesus." Her arms flew upward and she caught at the stair rail. Cans clattered to the floor and oranges rolled between Risa's feet. She couldn't speak.

The blonde rushed out of the kitchen. "What's the matter?" she asked. "What happened?"

Beatrice paid no attention to her. The brown eyes never left Risa's. "You can't be here," she said. "You're dead. Dead and buried."

17

2

Risa stared in disbelief at Beatrice. She couldn't speak. Her head throbbed and she clutched the back of a chair.

"What are you talking about, Bea?" the blond girl asked. "Are you saying this is Rory's sister? The one who was killed?"

Rory, Risa thought. Where's Rory? I've got to see him. This is a nightmare. "Where is he?" she demanded. "Where's Rory?"

The blond's answer seemed evasive to Risa. "I'm waiting for him to come back," she said. "Are you really Risa MacArthur? What . . . ?"

Risa ignored her question. "Beatrice," she said, turning to the other woman, "where's Rory?"

"He's gone."

"Where?"

"He didn't tell me. Never does tell me, you ought to know that." Beatrice took a deep breath and walked over to Risa. She reached out her hand to touch Risa's shoulder as if to make sure she was flesh and blood.

"Whatever happened? How could such a mistake be made?" she asked Risa. "Mr. Rory had to go down to Mexico and identify you. I mean he had to go look at the — the body. He thought the girl was you. It was his car in the accident and

18

you were supposed to be driving his car."

"I don't understand," Risa said. "I don't know anything about an accident." She put her hand to her head and swayed on her feet. "I've got an awful headache. I can't think."

"You better go on up to your room and rest, Miss Risa. Best thing you could do is — Oh, dear heavens, I forgot. Miss Allegra here is staying in your old room."

Risa frowned, not quite understanding.

Beatrice shook her head. "We thought you were — were dead and so Mr. Rory had me to pack up your things and . . ."

"I'll use one of the guest rooms. It doesn't matter right now."

"I suppose you're wondering about me," the blond girl said. "I'm Allegra Cortez, Rory's fiancée."

"You're engaged to Rory?" Risa took a step toward her. "He never mentioned . . ."

"How could he?" Allegra shrugged. "You've been gone a year."

"I don't know what you mean? Why couldn't he tell me? What are you saying about a year?"

"The funeral — well, the accident — was last November, a year ago. So how could he tell you? Everyone thought you were dead."

"A year ago?"

"Miss Risa, you haven't been home for a year," Beatrice told her. "Not since the accident and all."

Risa closed her eyes. I won't faint, she told herself, won't whirl off into darkness to discover I'm somewhere else entirely. That's crazy, what am I thinking? I'm here in my house. Rory's house. They have made some mistake. Beatrice and this Allegra. Allegra Cortez who says she's Rory's fiancée. Rory would not marry without telling me — she must be lying. A year? How could a year pass when I have no memory of it? This is November, I'm twenty-one this month, I can't be twenty-two, a year gone and I don't know how or where . . .

"I'll help you upstairs, Miss Risa." Concern underlined Beatrice's words. "You sure don't look too good."

"Why is she staying here?" Risa asked as Beatrice opened the door to the larger of the two guest bedrooms. "Why is that girl in this house?"

Beatrice stood back from Risa, her dark eyes widening in surprise. "She told you already. Mr. Rory wanted her to have a place to stay. He asked her."

"Is she homeless then?" Risa could hear the dislike edging her words and knew Beatrice could too.

"Well, Miss Allegra comes from Mexico. I don't know about her folks or anything."

"Doesn't she have any money?"

"Miss Risa, I don't ask questions like that. All I know is Mr. Rory asked me to take care of his little girl."

That's me, Risa thought, not Allegra. I used to be Rory's little girl. "I don't want her here."

Beatrice's brown face became blank, all trace

of emotion wiped away. "I can't go against Mr. Rory. You ought to know I can't." Then her face softened. "I know you're all upset, and no wonder, poor child. You just wait until Mr. Rory comes home and he'll straighten things out."

"When will he be here. Where is he?"

"I told you, I don't know."

"*She* must — his so-called fiancée."

"Miss Risa, why are you taking on so against Miss Allegra? She hasn't hurt you any."

"She's lying. Rory wouldn't get married without telling me."

"They're not married yet and how could he tell you anything at all with us thinking you were dead? Where've you been this whole year?"

"I — I had some problems." Safer not to admit to the loss of a year, not even to Beatrice. I don't want to think about the lost time yet, she told herself. I'm afraid to.

"Maybe you'll feel better when you have a little rest. Do you want some hot tea?"

"Nothing right now, Beatrice, thanks. I do feel awful." Impulsively she put her arms around the other woman and hugged her. "It's good to be home."

Was there a barely perceptible hesitation before Beatrice returned her hug? Risa wasn't sure.

"You go ahead and sleep, Miss Risa." Beatrice stared at her for a moment and Risa thought she saw a glint of fear deep in her brown eyes. Is she afraid of me? Risa wondered. Does she think I've returned from the dead? Risa half smiled, and shrugged. Now *I'm* getting macabre, she told herself.

But where had the year gone? Beatrice wouldn't lie, so it had been a year since she had last been in this house. A year of her life behind her with no recollection of how she had lived, what she'd done. How could it be? She knew her name, where she lived. Wait — she didn't know why she had been in the hospital parking lot earlier today. Had she been ill? A tendril of fear grew in her thoughts. Mentally ill? If only her head didn't hurt so much maybe she could remember.

She went into the bathroom and dampened a washcloth with cold water, returned to the bed and laid the cloth across her closed eyes.

Yesterday she had been in Mexico with Rory. Only it wasn't yesterday. A year ago, that was when they'd taken the trip, she and Rory. "I'm going to run down to Baja for some deep-sea fishing. Come along. If you don't want to fish you can lie in the sun, maybe swim."

She had been surprised and pleased.

"I may want to sail the boat up here to San Diego. You could drive the car back for me," Rory added.

Not quite so pleasing. But at least Rory wanted her company. She thought about them planning the trip to Baja, she and Rory. She could see him the day they left, behind the wheel of his Ferrari, eyes and hair with the same coppery sheen as the finish on his car. Her handsome brother.

He was not really her brother, of course. Actually, not even a stepbrother, because it was her aunt who married Rory's father when Risa was fourteen and Rory twenty-two. Aunt Marie, who had raised Risa, the only mother she could really remember . . .

Risa seemed to be lying in the sand while the sun rose brown and threatening behind the fog. The water came up to her, gray and sullen, reaching out for her but not quite touching. The sand was cold and dampness seeped into her as she waited. Someone would come. But meanwhile the sun spilled out rays of the wrong color, golden brown, hurting her eyes so she put her hands up, but, then it wasn't the sun, no, and she was not lying on the sand. She crouched on the rocks, holding the topaz brooch in her hand. Its stone was the color of the resin Aunt Marie used on her violin bow, a clear warm brown. It was the topaz glowing, warming her, but even as she stared the brooch was gone and there was danger on the cliff above her, someone calling her name. She must run . . .

Risa woke. For a moment she thought she was still in the dream with the ocean below her, the bluff above. But then she knew she was awake, outside her own Del Mar home, partway down the steep path to the beach. How did I get here? she thought in panic. Have I started to sleepwalk again? The fright of waking up and being somewhere without knowing she had walked in her sleep was an old, familiar terror, but none the less real.

There was no one in sight. On Aunt Marie's ranch in the San Joaquin Valley when she was a child, she would awaken in the sycamore grove and the moon would be shining, changing the tree trunks to white ghosts. Sometimes she woke thinking someone had called her but she was always alone. She was alone now, with the sun almost set and the chill evening breeze making her shiver.

Sleepwalking. But I couldn't have lost a whole year that way, she told herself. What had happened between the time she got into Rory's Ferrari and started off for Mexico on a sunny and cool day in November and this strange return in another November? Why had she found herself in the parking lot of Sharp Hospital with time and memory missing?

Risa was cold. Aunt Marie was no longer alive to come running across the field to the sycamore grove after the child Risa had been sleepwalking. She was alone now except for Rory. The thought of going back to the house was oppressive and yet she would need her coat if she wanted to walk along the beach. She had left it laying across the bottom of the bed. And there's five hundred dollars in an envelope in the pocket, she thought.

Why would I be carrying five hundred dollars? I couldn't have stolen the money — I wouldn't do that. Had Rory given the money to her? But, no, he thought she was dead, had buried her.

The accident was in Mexico, Beatrice said. Did the accident have something to do with Risa driving the Ferrari back alone while Rory brought the boat up to a San Diego mooring? But I didn't drive the car — surely I'd remember, Risa assured herself.

Who is buried in my grave? The thought prickled the hair on her neck. Someone died, some other girl, it had to be a girl because Beatrice said Rory identified the body. Whose body? How could he make such a mistake?

Risa began to pick her way along the path toward the beach despite the growing darkness and the damp ocean breeze. She couldn't face the house where she no longer even had a room of her own, was displaced by Allegra. Did Rory really mean to marry her?

He won't want me living with them, she thought. Where will I go? But that's silly. Rory doesn't even know I've come back, still thinks I've been killed. If he was home now I could talk to him, he would help me. Maybe he's waiting up there now.

She heard the rattle of small stones above her. Could that be Rory now, looking for her? "Rory?" she called. Silence. "Who's there?" she asked. Suddenly she was afraid. Someone was on the path between her and the house, someone who didn't answer. The urge to get away that she had felt earlier in the day came back to her. *Run* . . .

Risa slid down the path toward the beach, half

falling, sending dirt and rocks hurtling ahead of her. The darkness was deeper when she reached the sand and she hesitated a moment before starting up the beach. A shower of stones fell beside her and she began running.

There's nowhere to go, she thought in terror. I'll have to climb again to get to the road. But she kept going, blood pounding in her ears so she couldn't bear if there was a pursuer. Something touched her legs, lunged heavily against her and she screamed as she fell sideways, screamed as the wet furry muzzle thrust into her face.

Then she was rolling sideways, trying to get to her feet, striking out at the animal. She expected to feel teeth in her flesh but finally realized the dog was licking her instead, lavishing affection on her reluctant body.

She stood up and the dog pushed its head against her side. She touched its face with her hands. Long silky ears, pointed muzzle, a big dog. It whined happily.

He likes me, she thought. How strange, a dog coming out of nowhere, a dog I've never seen before and he likes me. Risa began to retrace her steps. She could see the lights of the house above her and thought she could make out the path going up. The dog stayed close beside her, she could feel his wet nose against her hand now and again as though he was checking on her.

She started up the path before the next thought hit her. This dog knows me. Why would he be so happy to see me and so protective now if he didn't? But we have never had a dog. Had Rory gotten one? But even if he had, the dog wouldn't know me.

Was this something from the lost year? How had the dog found her?

A short sharp whistle sounded, rose in pitch, stopped, sounded again. Risa could not tell where it came from but the dog vanished. She froze in apprehension against the side of the bluff but heard nothing else. After a few moments she ventured to climb again, darting frightened glances into the darkness around her. Who had called the dog? Was someone waiting for her at the top of the path? "Who — who's there?" she called, her voice thin with tension.

"Is that you, Risa?" A woman's voice, not Beatrice.

"Allegra?"

"Thank goodness. Bea is beside herself, convinced you'd disappeared permanently. Why didn't you tell us you were going for a walk on the beach?"

Risa struggled up the last few feet onto level ground. Allegra was at the top of the path, all the lights were on outside the house. There was no sign of a dog.

"I — it was an impulse," Risa said. "Is there anyone else here? I met a dog."

"I didn't see anybody," Allegra said.

They walked up the redwood steps to the lower deck and the yellow patio lights turned Allegra's blond hair to gold. Risa's hand went up to finger her own short curls and she winced as she touched the left side of her head. Sore. She must have hit it when the car knocked her down.

"Allegra," she said, "where's Rory?"

"He'll probably call sometime this week," Allegra said. "His business takes him all over."

"What business?" Risa asked. "He doesn't work."

"A year makes quite a difference," Allegra said, her voice cool. "Don't you agree?" And Risa knew the dislike was mutual.

Beatrice met them just inside the door. "Miss Risa," she said, "you had a phone call."

Risa swallowed. "Who — who from?"

Beatrice shook her head. "It was some man. Just asked if you were here and I said yes and then he hung up in my ear."

❧ 3 ❧

When Risa awoke in the morning she lay in bed for a while, letting her thoughts drift, reluctant to dress and go out to face the day. Aunt Marie would scold her if she were still alive. "Always dreaming, dreaming your life away. Just like your mother . . ."

Risa had only a vague memory of her mother, only one clear picture ever came to her — a woman promising her something, a present. A present that never came.

"She's gone, left you for me to raise," Aunt Marie said. "Likely she's dead so don't cherish the hope she'll come for you because she won't. Selfish. My own sister but selfish to the bone."

Marie would talk about Risa's mother sometimes, recollecting happier times when they had been the MacArthur Sisters and played their violins to audiences all over the state. But Aunt Marie would not tell Risa anything at all about her father except that he was dead. She grew angry, pursing her mouth in distaste when Risa asked.

Aunt Marie was almost a caricature of the old-maid school teacher, so it had been a surprise to Risa when her aunt married Steve Robertson. Steve Robertson with his handsome son, Rory.

And where was Rory now? Was there some

reason Allegra didn't want her to know where he was? Risa felt an uneasiness that drove her from the bed. Has something happened to Rory? she wondered as she hurried through her shower.

The robe borrowed from Allegra was too long for Risa and she stumbled on the steps, hitching up the robe with irritation, and mourned all the clothes Beatrice had packed up a year ago and given away. A strange feeling to realize you were officially dead. I wonder what I should do about that? she asked herself. Someone in authority should be notified. But who?

"I washed your things," Beatrice told her when she came into the kitchen. "You sure got them dirty. I couldn't get the shoes to looking right, though."

Risa thanked her and sat down at the table, where Allegra toyed with a cup of coffee. Allegra's bright blue eyes flashed from one to the other. She was pretty, Risa had to admit, with an immediate beauty you noticed as soon as you saw her. Rory could have his choice of women, but Risa hadn't thought he had ever had a special one — a girl he wanted to marry.

"Any news from Rory?" Risa asked. Both the other women shook their heads. "You're sure he wasn't the man who called me last night?" she persisted.

"Now Miss Risa, you know I'd recognize Mr. Rory's voice right off," Beatrice said. "I told you the man hung up. Why would Mr. Rory do that?"

But who would know I was here? Risa asked

herself again as she had the night before. The phone is listed under Rory Robertson. Anyway, I'm dead. She shivered suddenly despite the warmth of the kitchen.

The dog knows I'm alive, she thought. And how about the person who whistled for him? She glanced at Allegra. Was it possible Allegra had called the dog and hidden him, then come back to the top of the path? Had there been time? But why? And where was the dog now? It certainly had not been Allegra on the phone . . .

"Are you planning to stay here?" Allegra's voice was sharp.

"Why?"

"Well, I wondered. After all, you must have quite another life now, after a year away . . ."

It's not your place to wonder, Risa said to herself. I belong here as much as you do. More. But did she? Had Rory ever treated her with more than the amused tolerance he had first shown for the fourteen-year-old who thought he was wonderful? San Diego had been a change from the conservative small town in the San Joaquin Valley where she had lived with Aunt Marie. Rory had not thought of her as a real sister, maybe, but he had taken her to the beach and his friends there had liked her. One had taught her to surf, another to sail. It was just that he was so handsome, so much in demand, he didn't have time to spend with a kid, a teenager.

After all, when Steve Robertson, his father, died just a few months after they were married

31

— Rory had insisted she and Aunt Marie stay. Of course, Marie had been left the house and half the money, but just the same it was comforting to know Rory wanted them. Aunt Marie went out of her way to see he had everything he needed. She felt as Risa did about Rory — he *was* wonderful. If he was here, Allegra wouldn't be so — so . . .

"Miss Allegra, I think Miss Risa isn't feeling too good yet." No mistaking the warning in Beatrice's voice. Beatrice had been here when Risa and Marie came, Beatrice would be on her side.

Aunt Marie would have been able to handle Allegra. But Marie had been dead for — how long? Just a few weeks before the trip to Baja. A year ago.

I have no place to go, Risa thought in sudden panic. I have no money — Marie gave what little she had left to Rory, saying in the will it was his father's money. I have nothing. No one. Except Rory.

"Did you give everything away, Beatrice?" she asked. "All my things?"

Beatrice nodded. "Sorry, Miss Risa. But . . ."

What was it she almost remembered, something on the edge of her mind like a word on the tip of her tongue? "Was there anything valuable, anything Rory kept?"

"No, not that I know of. He told me to pack it all and I did. You had some costume jewelry I gave to my sister's girl. I can get that back if you want."

Jewelry — yes, a jewel, the brown glow. "Was there a topaz brooch?"

"Oh, no, Miss Risa. All I found was beads and like that. There wasn't any real jewels. I never saw you wear any brooch. That's like a pin, isn't it? No, you never had a topaz pin I knew of."

But the brooch was there, clear in her mind, the golden brown of the topaz set in engraved gold with enameling, the enamel the same color as the stone. An old brooch, the gold pin bent with age. Did it belong to her lost year?

"Rory gave me an emerald for an engagement ring," Allegra said. "Maybe you noticed." She thrust her left hand in front of Risa. The gem was square cut, a beautiful brilliant green. "I was born in May," Allegra said. "It's my birthstone. Were you born in November?"

"Why?"

"You were talking about a topaz brooch. That's a November birthstone."

"Yes, my birthday is this month, the twentieth." As she spoke Risa realized she was not sure of today's date. It had been the eleventh of November when she and Rory left for Baja. A year ago. "What's today's date?" she asked.

"Friday the thirteenth," Beatrice said. "Unlucky."

The thirteenth of November. Topaz, the gem for a November birthday. Had it been a present last year on her birthday? Why couldn't she remember?

"Topaz is lucky," Allegra said. "It protects

against sudden death."

There was a silence. Risa looked from Allegra to Beatrice, from the blue eyes to the brown. Neither met her gaze. She pushed away her unfinished coffee and stood up.

"I'm going to walk on the beach," she said. "Please let me know if Rory comes home."

Her car coat still had the envelope of money in the pocket. She put the coat on over the same clothes she'd worn yesterday, now clean and fresh, thanks to Beatrice. She went out the front way so she could go along the top of the bluff, where there was an easier descent to the ocean. As she walked, she watched for the dog. What kind was he? she wondered. Not a shepherd or boxer, not with those long ears she had felt last night. But no dog appeared.

She stood for a time and stared out over the ocean. A fog bank hovered offshore but the sun was out, shining dimly through a thin overcast. The beach beneath her was deserted, no birds scouted the sand for food, nothing moved except the eternal wash of the waves. Instead of soothing her, the emptiness made her clench her hands inside the pockets of her coat. She felt the roughness of the scabs on her palms and made a small sound of protest. Something else she didn't remember — how her hands had been injured.

Wooden steps had been fitted into the bank and she went down them to the beach, walking north until the rising tide covered the rocky outcropping and she had to turn back. I'll go up our private path, she thought. Maybe Rory is home by now.

As she neared the path, she saw she was no longer alone on the beach. A man squatted by the path, drawing designs in the sand with a stick. She came closer and saw he didn't have a stick at all, but a knife. Her step faltered.

"Kitty."

"Who are you?" she said, trying not to show fright.

She was near enough to see his eyes widen as she spoke. He gazed at her blankly and she decided to walk past him. High on something, she thought. Maybe I can . . .

"You found the money, didn't you?"

Risa kept moving.

"Damn it, Kitty, I know you have the money. That's all I want." She felt his hand on her wrist, then he wrenched her around so she faced him. "Always so aloof, playing the lady."

She stared into a bearded face, into pale blue eyes. She was looking at a man she had never seen before. "Let me go," she said, uneasily aware of the knife in his other hand.

"I don't want to hurt you. You know I could have. Last night and before that, too. Who would have known? But I didn't, I changed my mind. All I want is the money. I don't mean you any harm."

"What — what money?"

"The five hundred."

35

The envelope. Risa reached her free hand into her pocket and took out the envelope.

"That's it, yes." He dropped her wrist and jerked the money from her hand. She watched him look inside the envelope before he stuffed it in the pocket of his denim shirt. He flipped the knife shut, put it in his jacket. Then he turned his back to her and began to walk away, going south along the beach.

Risa took a step after him. "Wait," she called. "Wait a minute." But he increased his pace until he was running.

I can't catch him, she thought in despair. And he knew me. He called me "Kitty" but he knew me.

When she got to the top of the path, she hurried into the lower level, ran up the two flights of stairs inside the house and out the front door. Maybe the bearded stranger had parked along the bluff. If he had she might find him getting into his car.

She didn't see him. Instead, she saw Allegra alighting from a sports car at the end of the drive. As the car spun away the pale sun gleamed on the metallic sheen of the finish. Was it copper? Rory? But the Ferrari would have been wrecked if there had been an accident . . .

"Rory," she called uselessly, running up the drive. The car and its driver were gone before she even got close. "Why didn't he wait?" she gasped as she came up to Allegra. "Why didn't you make him wait? You know I have to see Rory."

"But that wasn't Rory," Allegra said, her blue eyes wide. Even in her distress, Risa couldn't help noticing how exactly they matched her Pucci pants.

"You're lying," Risa said. "The car was his color, you're hiding him from me." She began to cry. "Rory, Rory," she sobbed.

Allegra grasped her shoulders and shook her. "Stop that, Risa. I tell you it wasn't Rory. You're acting very odd. Anyone would think you had a mental problem. First you don't show up for a year, letting everyone think you're dead. Now you accuse me of keeping Rory away from you. Don't you think you're a bit paranoid?"

Risa wiped at her tears with the back of her hand. "Who were you with then?"

Allegra sighed. "Frankly, what I do is none of your business. He's a friend. You don't have to know who he is."

"Does he have a beard?"

Allegra stared at her. "You are really weird," she said. "As a matter of fact, no, he doesn't. Satisfied?"

I don't believe anything she says, Risa thought. But her assurance that the car belonged to Rory faded.

"I'll tell you what I think," Allegra said. "I think you ought to go to a psychiatrist."

"No," Risa said and began to run again, back toward the house, away from Allegra.

She shut herself in the bedroom. I won't pay attention to anything Allegra says, she told herself. I'm not crazy. But she could hear the bearded man saying, "Kitty." Am I Kitty somewhere else? she wondered. Sometime else? What was my relationship with that man? Surely I would remember him if we had been close in any way. Wouldn't I? And wouldn't I remember the name Kitty?

I can't just sit here and wait. Perhaps if I went to Sharp Hospital I could find out why I was in the parking lot, trace my steps backward from there. I don't have a car but I could take a bus. She paused. If I had any *money* I could take the bus, the five hundred dollars is gone. I never have needed money. Aunt Marie always gave me whatever I wanted.

Her aunt's voice rang in her ears. "Majoring in music is all very fine, you have talent, though not enough ambition for a career. Do you ever plan for the future? What will you do if you ever need a job?" Risa had not needed to work when her aunt was alive. Now she did. But finding a job wouldn't give her the money right now, this minute.

She shrank from asking Beatrice to loan her any. How much would she need? When could she pay it back? And Allegra was out of the question. Everyone else thinks I'm dead, she said to herself. I would have to explain. How can you explain not being dead? I don't even know why I'm not, I can't remember, maybe I really am dead and don't remember — No, no, that's dangerous to think, you're not going mad, you don't need a doctor . . .

38

A doctor. Jim Halloway's hazel eyes looking at her. "Let me help," he had said, and she had refused. Now she knew she needed help. What would he think if she called him? Perhaps he could go to the hospital and find out if there was something there, something of her past. She shivered. I don't want to see Sharp Hospital again, she thought.

But what could she tell Jim Halloway? Was it safe to tell him she had lost a year of her life? He was a doctor, he would understand. Or would he understand all too well? Where did they put people with amnesia? In mental hospitals?

❧ 4 ❧

Risa's fingers were clumsy with nervousness as she dialed information. "Dr. Halloway," she said into the phone. "Jim — James, I guess. He's an M.D."

The office girl didn't want to put Risa through to him at first.

"But he asked me to call," Risa persisted.

"The doctor is with a patient. I'll have to put you on hold."

"All right. I'll wait." Risa's foot tapped nervously. When Jim was finally on the other end of the phone she couldn't speak with clarity.

"They think I'm dead," she cried. "I'm afraid. You said you'd help."

"Risa? This *is* Risa MacArthur?"

How formal he sounded. She tried to organize the words tumbling from her but they pushed past her lips uncontrollably. "Rory's not here and the dog . . . then the man with the beard . . ."

"Wait, Risa. Stop talking. Where are you?" Jim's voice was low and calm.

"At home — you know, in Del Mar. But . . ."

"I can be out to pick you up in about an hour. Will that do?"

"Yes, oh yes, Jim." But after Risa hung up, doubts crowded into her mind, jostling aside the relief she had felt when Jim promised to come.

Was he hurrying to Del Mar because he thought of her as a patient, hysterical, possibly on the verge of a breakdown? Would it be dangerous to tell him she had lost her memory? How could he ever believe what she had to tell him was true — death and dogs and men with knives?

But who else could help her? Rory wasn't here, Rory who would explain everything, give her attention, affection. Yes, he would, even with Allegra around. Was Allegra an enemy? Risa felt she was. Beatrice, of course, was loyal but she was disturbed by Risa's return from the grave.

Risa couldn't stay still. She wandered into the upper lounge to play the piano and discovered with a shock no piano was there. I know we had a piano, she told herself firmly. Rory must have sold it when I — when he — after the accident. The disappearance of the piano so unnerved her that she left the house long before the hour was up, going out quietly, without attracting any notice. She waited for Jim at the beginning of the drive.

"Okay," he told her once she was settled in the orange Porsche, "let's take one thing at a time. Who's Rory?"

"My — my brother. Well, more of a step-brother. He's not at the house and I can't find out where he is."

"Who is at the house? Do you have parents?" he asked as they drove away from the house.

"No. No, I don't have anyone except Rory and

he's not there. His — well, she says she's his fiancée — is staying there. And the housekeeper. That's all."

"Exactly who thought you were dead and why."

"They buried someone a year ago thinking she was me. Beatrice, the housekeeper, nearly collapsed when she saw me yesterday."

"Who buried this unknown woman?"

"Well — Rory, I guess."

"Wouldn't your stepbrother know you? How was he persuaded you were dead?"

"I don't know. Beatrice says there was an accident a year ago November. Rory's Ferrari was wrecked and — and I was supposed to be driving at the time."

"Were you?"

"I — no — well — I couldn't have been because I'm not dead, don't you see?"

"Are you telling me you don't know whether you were driving the car, you don't remember?"

Risa turned away from him, staring out at the green freeway signs. "I don't even know if I was in the car at all, much less driving."

"Tell me what your housekeeper said to you about the accident. And tell me what you remember about what happened before."

"Well, Rory wasn't in the Ferrari because he was sailing the boat back to San Diego. I remember we had gone down to Baja, to Ensenada, Rory to fish and I was supposed to drive the car back."

"But you don't know if you did."

Risa shook her head. "Beatrice says Rory had to go down to Mexico and — and identify the body."

"Do you recall being in Baja?"

Risa closed her eyes and looked at the picture in her mind. Rory's copper hair glinting in the sun, shining like the metallic paint on the Ferrari. She was in the lime green pants and top Aunt Marie had bought for her birthday, then hadn't lived to give her. Risa had found the package, all wrapped and beribboned in her aunt's closet after her death . . . Risa and Rory, heading for Ensenada in the copper Ferrari.

Without warning, the scene in her head shifted. Rocks, and the brooch in her hand, golden brown as though the sun's warmth dwelt within the topaz.

She opened her eyes. "I remember leaving for Baja with Rory. But nothing else — except maybe the topaz . . ."

"What topaz?"

"It's set in a brooch. I don't know where the topaz is now but I held it once . . ."

"And this was last November, this Mexican trip, a year ago."

Risa nodded.

"What happened to you during the past year?"

She did not answer, looking instead at her hands clenched together in her lap.

Jim's hand reached over and pressed hers briefly. "Don't be afraid to tell me."

43

She glanced sideways and their eyes met — his hazel, concerned, and hers brown and what? Lost? Frightened? She was both. "The year is gone," she said at last. "I can't return to last November. But it isn't amnesia, not really. I know who I am, where I live. I know everything except the one year." She grasped Jim's arm. "If only I could remember what happened."

"Amnesia simply means a loss of memory." His voice was neutral and Risa brought her hand back to her lap. "The loss can be for hours, days, or a lifetime. Amnesia doesn't necessarily mean forgetting who you are, though that's the popular conception. But if you have lost a year, are you sure you were Risa MacArthur throughout the missing time?"

She stared at him wide-eyed. "Who else would I be?"

"I don't know," he said. "Right now I'm taking you to Sharp Hospital."

"Oh, no, please," she begged. "Please don't think I'm crazy." She began to cry.

Jim's hand was on her arm. "Stop it, Risa."

She jerked away. "You think I'm losing my mind," she sobbed. "You want to put me in . . ."

"No. I said stop crying. If you'd listen before you react you'd save a lot of distress. What I was trying to say is, I found you in the parking lot at Sharp Hospital so let's see if we can't discover what you were doing there. You don't know, do you?"

She shook her head, digging a tissue from her

coat pocket to wipe her eyes.

"I suspected from the first you were confused."

"All I know is the car — that woman in the car — bumped me and I fell down. I remember I felt I had to get away from there, hurry and get away from you and the woman."

"Have you ever had amnesia before?"

"No."

"How about sleepwalking?"

"Oh, yes, I used to a lot. When I was little Aunt Marie worried about my sleepwalking."

"Tell me about it."

Risa took a deep breath and sat up straighter in the seat. An image of the old ranch house formed in her mind, the weather-aged redwood board and batten siding askew from missing nails, the cracked adobe fields surrounding the house hard and dry in the summer and a clinging muck during the rains.

"I grew up in the San Joaquin Valley," she told Jim. "We lived on a small ranch outside a town called Porterville."

"We?"

"My aunt Marie and I. We didn't have much money. She taught school and was always rather odd but I think she loved me. She tried to take good care of me."

"When did you begin to walk in your sleep?"

"I guess I always did. Aunt Marie used to scold me as far back as I can recall. 'If you'd just make up your mind not to, Risa, I'm sure this business

45

of nightwalking would stop.' " Risa's lips quivered into a half-smile. "She was a firm believer in mind over matter, in willpower. I was a disappointment to her in many ways."

"How about your mother?"

Risa shrugged. "I didn't know her. At least, not exactly." She paused, decided against telling Jim of her dreams. What did he care about dreams?

"And your father?"

"I was an illegitimate child."

"You've no idea who he was?"

Risa shook her head. "Aunt Marie must have hated him, even the mention of his name made her angry."

"So you do know his name."

"Tony, that's all. My mother called me MacArthur, it was her last name."

Jim had turned off the freeway and now Risa saw the white rise of Sharp Hospital before them. She hunched in her seat.

"I'm afraid."

Jim pulled the Porsche into a DOCTORS ONLY parking slot and turned to her. "Of what?"

"I don't know — afraid to go inside. Like something terrible is waiting in there. I can't explain the feeling."

But she got out of the car and Jim grasped her arm firmly. "We have to start somewhere," he said.

Risa tried to walk calmly, but as Jim steered her toward the door marked EMERGENCY

ENTRANCE she began to tremble. He tightened his hold on her arm and continued on into the building.

"Let me wait in the car while you ask," she said.

"I want the E.R. nurses to see you. Sometimes the sight of a face will trigger recall."

Risa averted her eyes from the rooms along the corridor, tiny rooms. Were there people in those rooms? Emergency cases, accident victims? She wouldn't look. "My headache's coming back," she told Jim.

He kept walking, pulling her along, until he found the charge nurse. He began talking to her.

"No, I don't recognize her, doctor. You can ask the clerk to check yesterday's patient roster."

Jim found no Risa MacArthur had been treated in the E.R. Nor had anyone of that name been a patient in the hospital yesterday.

Risa sighed in relief when they went back outside in the November sunlight.

Jim shook his head. "I still think the hospital is involved in this but I can't decide what else to check."

"Let's go," Risa urged.

"Where? Do you want to go back to Del Mar?"

"No." She stopped and looked at Jim.

"I want to help you," he said, "but I don't know where to begin. Do you have any memories at all from the past year?"

"I don't think so. Could I have been at the old ranch, is that why I see it in my mind so clearly?

And I remember the topaz brooch. Do you think the ranch and the topaz are connected?"

"Do they go together in your mind?"

"I — I can't be sure."

Jim touched the side of her face softly. "You're so forlorn," he said. "Don't worry. We'll find out. This is my weekend off call. I can drive you up to the San Joaquin Valley if you want to go. Maybe seeing the ranch itself will bring something back."

"Yes! I'd like to go. I haven't been there in years." She paused, then went on. "At least I don't think so, I don't remember."

"I have to be in the office tomorrow morning so we'll wait until Sunday. Then we can leave early, have the whole day. Okay?"

Risa nodded. "I'm so glad you're helping me," she said. "I didn't know what to do."

He studied her face for a moment. "I have to take you home soon," he said. "I'm on call to-night. But how about lunch tomorrow? Rather late, I'm afraid, maybe between one-thirty and two o'clock. Don't dress up — maybe we'll do something afterwards."

"I'd like to have lunch with you."

"Good. I'll pick you up as close to one-thirty as I can make it."

On the way back Risa realized she didn't want to go to the Del Mar house for the night. It didn't seem like her home without Rory there. Still, where else was home? "Drop me off on the road, by the driveway," she said after they were on the freeway. I'll wait there tomorrow for you, too."

"No. I'd like to meet your housekeeper and the other girl staying there — your stepbrother's fiancée."

"But they — they don't know about my lost year."

Jim went on as though he hadn't heard. "And perhaps your stepbrother will be back. I'd like to talk to him."

So would I, Risa thought. Oh, Rory, where are you? "He won't be there," she said to Jim, her voice positive. "Allegra doesn't want me to see him, I know she doesn't."

"Is Allegra the girlfriend?"

"Yes."

"I gather she's a stranger to you and vice versa."

"I never saw her before yesterday."

Jim stopped the car in front of the house. He's checking on me, Risa thought suddenly. He doesn't believe what I told him about Beatrice thinking I was dead. She clenched her teeth together, but got out of the car and led him into the house and down to the kitchen.

"Miss Risa." Relief combined with irritation edged Beatrice's voice. "I didn't know where you'd gotten to."

"This is Jim Halloway, Beatrice. He's a — a friend of mine."

Beatrice acknowledged the introduction, then turned again to Risa. "Miss Allegra's been worried and so have I."

"About what?"

"You didn't say where you were going and I couldn't find you for lunch. I guess I think you'll disappear."

"Is Risa back? Is that who you're talking to, Bea?" Allegra came down the stairs to the lower level. She had changed to a long dress, a blue chiffon that floated in back of her, the color again chosen to match her eyes. Risa felt scruffy in her soiled shoes and undistinguished coat and pants. I'm so drab, she thought. She glanced at Jim and saw his open admiration of the vision drifting down the stairs.

"This is Allegra Cortez," Risa said, her voice flat, as devoid of feeling as she could make it. "Jim Halloway."

Now you've met them, Risa said silently to Jim, watching Allegra maneuver him up the steps and into the living room while Risa trailed behind.

"I'm a doctor," she heard Jim say in answer to a murmured question.

Risa's dislike of Allegra expanded. She's deliberately keeping her voice down, Risa thought, so he has to lean close to her to hear. Just a cheap trick. But who could compete with Allegra's shining blond hair, the perfect heart-shaped face and those wide blue eyes?

He likes me, I know he does, Risa told herself, once again feeling the touch of Jim's fingers on her cheek. I'm not merely a patient to him, an interesting case . . . She watched Allegra link her

50

arm with Jim's, draw him across the room to see the view of the ocean.

I should be showing him, Risa thought. He bent over Allegra at the same time she turned her face up to him, and Risa tightened her mouth. Can't he see what she's up to? she wondered. Can't he tell she's doing all this deliberately? But her assurance of Jim's interest in herself faded as the pair continued to talk, excluding her. She walked across the room to stand beside them.

"Would you like something to eat?" she asked.

Jim's head turned toward her, almost reluctantly it seemed. "No thanks. You run along and have supper. I'll see you tomorrow."

How dare he dismiss her? And what right did this woman have in her house? Risa opened her mouth to speak but Allegra was already floating toward the front door, Jim in her wake.

"I just adore Porsches," she said. "I'd love to see yours."

Risa felt chilled. Allegra is my enemy, she thought. It's not a silly notion. She won't tell me where Rory is and now she is doing her best to distract Jim. Why?

೭ *5* ೭

Risa rose early. Beatrice had done her best with the shoes again but they were still scuffed, and though the clothes she must wear had been freshly laundered Risa was tired of them. I'll have to find a way to get some other clothes soon, she thought.

After her experience of the day before, she was reluctant to walk on the beach alone. She decided to go into Rory's room to see if she could find some indication of where he might be. Feeling like an intruder, she slipped through his door, closed it behind her. The room did not look like he had left permanently, it had an air of waiting, as though he would step inside the door any moment. Risa glanced over her shoulder but the door remained shut.

The same picture of Rory standing beside the Ferrari was on his dresser, no other pictures were in the room. None of Allegra, Risa thought with satisfaction. She took up the coppery frame and stared at Rory's face. Her heart contracted with the pain of missing him. He called me a pest, she thought, but he took me with him to Baja, trusted me to drive his car, his beloved Ferrari.

It was hard to remember the Ferrari was gone. Smashed on the rocks? she wondered. The Baja highway was largely rough rock along the shoulders. She hated to drive it.

She put the picture back and slid open his closet door. Most of his clothes seemed to be hanging there. Of course, he could have new ones — a year was a long time. But the closet was full of clothes. Surely he could not have taken many, wherever he had gone. That should mean he would be back soon. Why did she have this conviction he was being kept away so he wouldn't know she had come home, was alive?

His desk was locked. The dresser and chest of drawers were full of neatly folded underclothes and socks and handkerchiefs and scarves. He must be traveling light.

Risa felt a strong sense of frustration as though she ought to be able to understand what was going on if her mind would let her. There was a wall closing her away from what she needed to know. If only she could tunnel through to reach last year's memories, then magically Rory would be here too, everything all right.

She shook her head, took one last look around, and opened the door to leave. Allegra was standing in the hall.

"Checking up?" she asked, eyebrows raised.

"I — I wondered . . ." Risa's words trailed off. What was there to say?

"Did you think I had him locked in the closet?"

Since that was fairly close to the truth — that Allegra knew where Rory was and wouldn't tell her — she didn't reply.

"Are you going to see that good-looking doctor again today?"

Risa nodded.

"Be sure to bring him back with you. I find him utterly charming."

Not if I can help it, Risa thought. I don't intend to bring him anywhere near you.

"I'd wait and say hello to him," Allegra went on, "but someone's picking me up." She turned away and after a moment Risa heard her open and close the front door. She had an impulse to run after Allegra, follow her to see if she was going to Rory.

That's crazy, she told herself. Rory would come home if he could, he certainly would not be meeting Allegra someplace in secret. I'm getting paranoid like she said. She is probably going out with another man and doesn't want me to see — or Beatrice either.

Risa went to find Beatrice. "Do we — does Rory have any charge accounts I can use?" she asked.

Beatrice shook her head. "I don't know about that. All I know is Miss Allegra gives me the money to buy food and supplies for the house. If you're thinking about clothes, you could borrow some from Miss Allegra and I could fix them to fit you."

"No." Risa couldn't bear the idea of wearing Allegra's clothes. She tried to smile at Beatrice. "Thanks anyway. I'll figure something else out."

By the time Jim arrived, at one-forty, she was more than ready to leave the house. "I don't feel I belong here anymore," she told him. "But if not here, then where do I belong?"

"Don't brood about lost memories," he said. "Forcing yourself to remember anything is futile. You can't will missing time to return. Try to relax. Just drift along today, don't think at all. Okay?"

Risa nodded, hoping she would be able to, but doubtful.

They ate lunch at the Point Loma Inn. A long-haired waiter dressed in jeans perched on the edge of their table and asked how things went.

"So-so," Jim said. "Too early to tell, maybe."

"How about you?" The waiter looked at Risa.

"I — I don't know," she said.

The young man shrugged. "You'd better find out," he advised, moving away from their table.

"Do you suppose he wants to make us feel at home?" Jim said.

Risa smiled uncertainly. What people said to her seemed to have hidden meanings, she felt she missed what they really meant. She sipped at the drink she had ordered, a marguerita, licked the salt from her lips. Mexican, she thought, looking at her glass. Everything seems to point to Baja. And yet I keep thinking of the ranch.

"How old are you?" Jim asked.

"Twenty-one — no, twenty-two." She wondered how old he was but was shy of asking.

Thirty? Why wasn't he married?

"Do you know what we're going to do after we eat?" he asked.

"No."

"We're going out to Cabrillo Monument and see if we can spot any whales."

"It's a little early," she said. "December's more their month for migrating south."

He waved his glass at her. "Today there'll be some — just for us. Want to bet?"

"It's early for them," she repeated.

"Bet you a dime."

She shook her head. How could she tell him she didn't even have a dime to bet?

"The lighthouse is out there, isn't it?" she asked.

"Yes."

"I've never been inside it. Can I go inside?"

"Be my guest," he said. "Anything you want this afternoon is yours."

They drove past the Navy cemetery on their way out to the point, hundreds of white crosses so close it didn't seem there was room to have the bodies underneath. I'm supposed to be buried, she thought. I wonder where my grave is? Should I ask Beatrice? No, I'd only upset her. And I don't really think I would like to see it anyway. She shivered.

"Cold?"

"No, it's a lovely day."

The sun made the ocean sparkle so brilliantly she had to turn her eyes away. The side windows of the car were down and the air was fresh but not cold. "I'm glad I'm alive," she said suddenly.

"So am I," Jim said.

She glanced at him and he smiled at her, his hazel eyes warm and friendly. She smiled back. "You don't seem like a doctor today," she said.

"How does a doctor seem?"

"Oh, I don't know. Always wanting to find out if you've had measles and mumps."

"Have you?"

"No."

"Well, it's plain to see you're the healthy type, so I can relax." He turned the Porsche into the parking area. "Lighthouse first," he said. "Then the good gray whales."

In some obscure way the lighthouse was a disappointment to her. Maybe it was the colorful quilts on the bed, the cheerful hooked rugs on the floor. She had expected lonesomeness, a sense of solitary vigil. The interior of this lighthouse was positively homey. And crowded with sightseers.

Jim took her hand and led her toward the rocky point. "If we can't see anything here I'll drive the car down and we can climb out on the rocks." He had a binocular case hung around his neck by a strap and now he took out the glasses and handed them to her. "See anything?"

Risa scanned the waves, brought suddenly close by the binoculars. What was that? No, only a seagull — Wait, not a gull either, it was a pelican diving for fish. She watched the big bird until it flapped out of sight around the point.

"No fair! You're looking at the sky," Jim said. "How can I win my bet that way?"

She handed him the glasses. "You look."

He glanced around at the people on the point with them and said, "Let's go back to the car. I think the lower rocks are a better place today."

She watched the ocean as they wound down to the rocks. Was that a spout? Were there really whales out there now, headed already for the lagoons in Baja to have their babies? Baja again.

Out of the car, Jim took her hand to help her climb the rocks. He found a vantage spot where no one else was and pulled out the binoculars, put them to his eyes.

Risa looked down at the water but she no longer saw anything but her own images from within. The rocks, she climbed on the rocks. She used to climb the granite boulders at the ranch when she was a child, hide among them when her aunt came searching for her. "Time for your piano lesson," Aunt Marie would call. "I know you're in the grove, Risa MacArthur, and you'd better get out here quick."

Yet the boulders at the ranch were friendly. She remembered another time on the rocks, a time of danger and fear. She glanced over her shoulder now as though expecting to see a pursuer, and she moved closer to Jim.

He turned to her. "I give up. Can't spot a thing."

She took a deep breath and reached for the glasses. This is *now*, she told herself. I'm with Jim on these rocks and nothing is wrong. She gazed through the binoculars at the ocean and cried out with surprise and pleasure. One, two — no, three water spouts. And then she could see the massive backs of the whales coming up out of the water, rising . . .

"I see them, there's three of them, oh look Jim, you're right, there they are." She handed back the glasses.

When the whales submerged again, he took the glasses from his eyes and they grinned at each other. Risa felt an unreasonable elation.

Though they searched again from time to time, they saw no other whales. She sat on the rocks with Jim as the sun dropped lower in the sky. "I liked the afternoon," she said.

"Past tense?"

"No," she said hastily. "But I don't think you can top the whales."

"I don't intend to try. I'll tell you something — I like you, not merely the afternoon. You'll note I use present tense."

She looked into his eyes, saw the pupils widen and for a tense moment thought he was going to kiss her, but he raised his head and glanced quickly at his watch. "Getting late."

Risa didn't know if she was relieved or disappointed.

The sky was turning orange, shadows began to settle among the rocks. Risa became uneasy. She closed her hand, opened it, and felt tears prick her eyes when she gazed into her empty palm.

Jim rose to his feet and helped her up. Neither of them spoke as they walked back to the car.

"I don't want to give you up yet," Jim said, "but I promised one of the other doctors in the group I work with that I'd take his calls this evening. So I'll have to take you home."

She nodded.

"We'll start early tomorrow, it's a long drive to Porterville."

"Do you think I'll find anything, remember anything?"

Jim shrugged. "We won't know until we try. There doesn't seem to be anything else to go on."

The closer they came to Del Mar, the tenser Risa became. I don't want to stay in that house any longer, she thought. But what can I do? Jim's already done so much for me. "I wish . . ." she said, not realizing for a moment she had spoken aloud.

"You wish what?"

What had she wished? That Jim would take her somewhere far from Del Mar and they would have every day as pleasant as this afternoon had been. She couldn't tell him that.

"Oh, I wish it was a year ago and nothing had happened," she said.

"And you'd never met me?"

"I didn't mean not meeting you. I'm glad we met, but . . ."

"But you'd rather have your memories of the year back."

Not rather. Too. She couldn't say the words. I want to know about the year but I don't want to lose you.

Jim brought the car to a stop in front of the house and got out. He's going to come in again, she said to herself and her heart sank. Allegra would be home, he would see Allegra again.

Allegra was wearing the lavender pantsuit she had had on when Risa first saw her. "Oh, Jim," she said, ignoring Risa, "I hoped you'd come in." Allegra touched Jim's arm and he smiled down at her.

Risa felt shut out, excluded, the day dismissed as though it had never been.

"We're driving up to the San Joaquin Valley to-morrow," she said to Allegra. "I'll be leaving early."

Both Jim and Allegra looked at her, and Risa felt like a child who had interrupted her elders. She bit her lip and turned away.

"I have to go now," Jim said, but Risa didn't answer, didn't even turn back to watch him leave. She heard the front door close and glanced around. Allegra had gone outside with him.

Risa waited in the living room until Allegra returned.

"Such a charming man," Allegra said. "He's invited me to go along tomorrow when you go on your drive. Isn't that fun?"

Risa couldn't look at her. It was as though Jim had betrayed her, she thought, and now there was no one.

6

On the way to Porterville the next day, Risa spoke very little. Allegra had managed the seating so that Risa sat alone in the back. Sitting there with the two of them in front of her, she tried to shut out the sound of Allegra's high, tinkling laugh and Jim's amused responses.

Why did Allegra want to come? Not merely interest in Jim as a man, Risa was sure of that. Although he was nice-looking, he wasn't as handsome as Rory. Few men were. But Jim did have a way of making you feel you mattered. Or at least he had before. Now only Allegra seemed to interest him. If he was that taken with Allegra, why bother with this trip? Couldn't he simply have gone off somewhere else so he could be alone with her, not bother with me in the back seat, an unwilling observer.

I should have told him not to bother with me anymore. I should have told him when he came to pick us up. Then he and Allegra might have enjoyed the day without me. What good is going to the ranch anyway? I don't really remember being there last year. Why would I go there?

"Is that fog?" Jim asked, then repeated the question.

Risa realized he was speaking to her. They had come up over the Ridge Route and were about to descend into the San Joaquin Valley. She saw the gray wall ahead of them.

"Yes. Tule fog. About halfway down the Grapevine we'll be into it. I can remember the Valley fogs — they're not the same as we have in San Diego."

"That's silly," Allegra said. "Fog is fog."

"Wait. You'll see."

The car started down the long, twisting grade called the Grapevine toward the gray sea. Risa caught her breath as the first tendrils coiled about the car, recalling her fear as a child that the fog would choke her if she breathed it in, drift gray and formless within her until she smothered. When Jim switched on the headlights and the fog swirled on all sides, Risa imagined an inward pressure, almost as though the sides of the car were being squeezed.

She closed her eyes and tried to calm herself. I'm not a child, she said silently. This is sheer fantasy, I'm being silly, as Allegra said. Fog is fog. She kept her eyes closed until Jim asked her about the Porterville turnoff.

After they left the freeway, though the grayness crowded close, Risa knew they were driving through young orange groves and the land was gradually changing from the flat of the Valley to rolling hills. Soon they had passed Porterville and were climbing into the foothills of the Sierras. One moment they were shrouded by fog, the next moment the sun shone.

"We're above the fog," Risa said. She glanced

through the back window at the gray, alien sea behind.

Allegra had spoken less the last hour. "Ugh," she said now, "what unpleasant weather."

"The access road to the ranch is about a mile ahead on your left," Risa told Jim. "Then there's another few miles." She sat forward, eager to catch the first familiar glimpse.

There. The twisted oak growing almost horizontal to the ground before sending out upreaching branches. The sign pointing to the Indian Reservation. The tree farm, with all the different-sized evergreens — CHOOSE YOUR OWN LIVING CHRISTMAS TREE.

"That's the drive up ahead. Turn left." The driveway was rutted and dead weeds poked up through the scattered gravel. When they came close to the house, Risa caught her breath. "Oh, no!"

"Why the place is in ruins," Allegra said. "Surely you couldn't have lived here."

"I can't believe Aunt Marie would have let this happen," Risa said. "The house needed repairs when we lived in it but nothing like now." She looked at the caved-in roof, the broken windows, the front door askew on one hinge.

"How many years since you've lived here?" Jim asked.

"Seven — no, eight." I couldn't have been here last year, Risa thought. No one could live in the house anymore.

"Let's look around," Jim said.

64

Risa stood on the rotting porch and stared through the open door. All gone, the paraphernalia of her childhood. Had her aunt sold the furniture when they left? Certainly they had brought little enough from the ranch house to San Diego, as though Aunt Marie wanted to go unencumbered into their new life. Risa felt an aversion to entering, looking at the dying house any further. It made her wonder if her view of the past was as distorted as her mental picture of the ranch house put up against the reality in front of her.

"Come on inside," Jim said.

"You aren't afraid of old ghosts are you?" Allegra asked, laughing.

They went past her and through the doorway. She watched them. Allegra was already reaching for Jim's arm, crowding close to him.

Risa shook her head. No, they didn't want her and the house had nothing for her, not now. She turned and went down the steps, around the side of the house and across an unplowed field.

Goatheads, the ubiquitous tiny pronged burrs she recalled from childhood, clung to her pant legs and fastened themselves in her shoes. She'd be hours picking them out. At the end of the field was the cluster of sycamores, exactly as before, with the massive granite boulders separating the trees, some stones so huge they rose above the brown-leafed sycamores. The stream was a mere trickle, not yet fed by the winter rains.

Risa stopped, leaned against one of the boulders and ran her hand over the roughness of the granite. The spot both attracted and repelled her. She had described it to Rory many times, telling him how she was drawn here even in her sleep, how she would wake and find herself among the trees — the white trunks of the syca- mores eerie in the moonlight, the rocks masses of darkness. And, awakening, she would think someone had been here with her, whose words were still in her head, important words she never remembered.

She had told Aunt Marie about her dreams in the grove when they still lived at the ranch and her aunt grew pale and tightened her mouth. "You must stop this nightwalking, the grove is no place to be at night, haunted as it is by the past."

"Ghosts?"

But Aunt Marie told her not to talk foolishly. Of course, there were no ghosts, the past lived only in the minds of living people. Risa was too young then to know what her aunt meant.

Risa gazed now at the huge rocks with the trees scattered randomly among them. Were these the rocks she saw when she remembered the topaz brooch? Was the topaz somehow connected with her mother and the sleepwalking dreams of the past? She leaned her head back and closed her eyes, trying to bring the image into her mind. Rocks and the topaz . . .

Gold-brown, the brooch in her hand, and she herself standing on the rocks looking down at the water. A sense of danger, of death . . .

Risa opened her eyes, shaking off the anxiety. The boulders here were not connected with danger and the small stream wasn't the water lapping below the rocks in the image in her mind. Whatever this spot had meant to her in childhood was lost, there was no use dallying here. Probably Jim and Allegra were more than ready to leave.

But as Risa circled the rock she recalled the path she used to follow, the ritual way of returning to the ranch from the grove. "I had to go exactly the same way each time," she had told Rory once, "or I'd never break out of the dark enchantment that kept me from taking my rightful place." Rory had shrugged and told her he supposed all orphans felt they were mistreated in one way or another. He did not have much use for flights of fancy.

Risa determined to follow the old path yet one more time, just the same. Around the rock, to the left of the tree, climb over the next boulder, to the right, now the left . . . The turnings of the invisible path were as clear to her as they had been in the past. Now the wooden planks came next, over what Aunt Marie said was an old well. The planks were solid, but Risa used to persuade herself she heard a hollow echo as she crossed over the unseen opening, adding spice to her venturing. The planks should be about here, but where were they? Was she wrong?

She thought she heard a shout. Was Jim calling her? Abandoning the idea of following her secret path, she began to hurry, trying to see through the trees whether Jim was coming across the field.

Then she was stumbling, falling, the ground opening beneath her. She scrabbled in panic at the weeds, the dirt, and finally clutched a sycamore seedling that bent in her grasp but remained rooted. Her legs hung in a hole, she was suspended in space, only her hold on the young tree prevented her from dropping down into whatever unknown chasm lay beneath.

Risa screamed again and again. Even in her terror, as her hands slipped along the smooth trunk of the seedling, she thought of the old well and knew she had stumbled into the opening.

"Jim," she called. "Help!"

She sobbed in desperation, knowing she couldn't hold on much longer. Where were the wooden planks, why wasn't the well covered as it always had been? She felt the tree begin to give, the roots coming up from the ground and closed her eyes. When a hand covered hers she couldn't believe it. The hand slid down her arm, gripped firmly.

"Push against the side of that hole with your feet." Jim's voice, low, tense with urgency. "Climb up with your feet while I pull on your arms."

Risa jammed her feet against the side nearest her and felt hardness under them. She tried to force her toes into a niche and something gave, fell underneath her to land with a clunk on whatever lay below.

"You must let go of the tree," Jim told her. "One hand at a time. Grasp my wrist."

"I'll pull you in, we'll both fall," she sobbed.

"I'm holding on to a branch with my other hand. Do as I say. Grab my arm and push with your feet."

Risa pushed as hard as she could, trying to climb upward with her feet while her hands clutched Jim's wrist. In a moment she lay half out of the hole, then all out, prone on the ground, face pressed into the dirt. Jim helped her to sit.

"Are you all right?"

She nodded. "I — It's the old well," she said. "But there were boards across before . . ."

Jim went past her to peer into the cavity. "Oh, my God," he said.

Risa crept on her hands and knees to look, too. In the bottom of the hole she saw two prongs, twisted and curved so they pointed upward. Something about them seemed familiar, something to do with the ranch, with farming . . .

"Why that's an old hay fork," she said. "It was on a machine and they used to pick up the bundles of hay with it. I remember watching." She stared at the implement. "But the fork is broken. The prongs are all twisted out of shape — they wouldn't stick up like that. Why I could have . . ." Her words trailed off and she edged away from the hole.

"Yes." Jim's voice was grim. "You could have been impaled."

Risa scrambled to her feet and grasped at Jim's arm, tugging him away from the opening. "Let's go," she urged.

But he didn't move. "Was the hole always there?" Jim asked.

"Aunt Marie told me it was an old well. But there were planks nailed to posts driven into the ground, and they closed off the opening. I never saw the opening before." She shuddered. "It — it didn't used to be dangerous. I used to stomp on the planks when I was little to hear the hollow sound my feet made."

"The posts are still here," Jim said, "but the boards are gone, no sign of them. We can't leave this the way it is."

Risa nodded, agreeing with him. I might have been killed except for Jim, she thought. I would really have been dead this November instead of last.

Allegra was in a poor humor as she waited with Risa while Jim went into town to get help. "What a waste of a day this was," she said.

"You didn't have to come," Risa couldn't prevent herself from saying.

Allegra brushed at her emerald green pants, smudged with dirt, and picked goatheads from the cuffs. Risa looked away, staring down the drive. When she turned back, Allegra was watching her, blue eyes intent.

"What's the matter?" Risa knew she was a mess, with stains covering her clothes and probably her face too. She licked her lips and tasted grit.

"Why are you still pretending?" Allegra said. "Don't you think I know anything?"

"I haven't any idea what you mean."

Allegra shrugged her elegant shoulders. "The poor little lost girl bit. I'll admit you do a fair job. Bea half believes you and Jim has been taken in, but I'm hard to con. What do you want?"

"I don't — I'm not . . ." Risa stared into Allegra's mocking smile. "Oh, what's the use of talking to you. If you'd only tell Rory I'm home, let me see him . . ."

Allegra widened her eyes and shook her head slowly. "But I don't know where Rory is. Naturally I'll tell him you're home as soon as he calls."

Risa wanted to strike out at the pretty face. Liar. Allegra was a liar.

Jim's orange car came up the drive followed by a tow truck. Jim parked the Porsche and Allegra immediately opened the door. "Let's go," she said.

But Jim got out and went over to the tow truck.

"I'm coming, too," Risa said and climbed into the truck cab after Jim.

"This is Hank Albers," Jim said. "We're going to pull the fork up out of the well."

"Pleased to meet you, Miss." The Porterville man was sandy-haired, face permanently reddened by the Valley sun. He drove his truck across the field and backed up to the well opening. They all got out and the two men gazed into the hole.

"This is part caved in," Hank Albers said, speaking with the familiar nasal twang Risa recalled from her childhood here. "Must of been a hell of a lot deeper once."

"Still deep enough to be dangerous," Jim said. He secured the rope ladder to a tree and threw the rungs into the hole. "Okay, give me the hook and try to fasten it when I can reach." He started down into the hole.

The hook was connected to a chain wound around a winch on the back of the truck. Hank unwound the chain a little, then went to the edge of the well.

Jim's head reappeared. "Wait a minute," he said. "I found something. It was sticking out of a hole in the side right up near the top." He handed an object to the other man, who put it on the ground and bent over the opening to watch Jim descend. Risa moved cautiously closer, still not liking to come close to the well but curious about what Jim had found. She saw it was a Mason jar and edged nearer until she could pick up the jar, then backed away. She was terrified lest Jim fall and yet she couldn't bring herself to watch.

Over near a boulder, Risa brushed at the dirt encrusted on the jar. She tapped the lid with her fingernail and heard the ping that meant the jar was firmly sealed. What was inside? Though it looked like paper, she couldn't be sure. She glanced at Hank. He was intent on Jim's progress, paying her no attention, and Jim was still inside the hole. She wrenched at the lid, twisting as hard as she could, but it stuck fast. Finally she smashed the jar against the boulder, then bent to pick an envelope from the glass shards. There was nothing else in the jar. She slid the envelope into her coat pocket just as Jim's head came into sight.

"All right," he said. "Let's try to yank that damned thing out of there."

The truck pulled away slowly and after a moment when nothing seemed to happen, the hay fork flew out of the hole, scattering dirt in all directions. The truck stopped, the man got out and unhooked his chain.

"Can't you haul it away?" Jim asked.

"Maybe tomorrow," Hank said. "Like I told you, I got to go up to the reservation and tow a guy into town. This'd just be in my way. I'll get back here, though, soon as I can and haul her off. Bring some boards, too."

"Well, I guess it can't do any damage sitting there," Jim said.

"Naw, won't hurt anyone now."

"Thanks for your help," Jim said.

"Easiest money I earned all week." The sandy-haired man started his truck and they watched him bump across the field, headed for the access road.

"Where's the jar?" Jim asked.

"I smashed it because I couldn't open it," Risa said. "But it was empty."

Jim looked at her, hazel eyes intent, and she

73

forced herself to meet his gaze. He shrugged and turned away. "Better start back," he said.

"Well, did you finally accomplish your good deed for today?" Allegra's high voice was snappish as they got into the car. She was in the back, so Risa sat next to Jim.

"Would you want someone killed?" Jim asked.

"Oh, don't be silly. Whoever would wander out to such a godforsaken spot?" Allegra spoke peevishly.

"I did," Risa said.

"Well, who else would? Honestly, this day has been beyond belief."

"I wonder how the hay fork got into the well?" Jim said.

"Obviously someone wanted to get rid of the thing," Allegra said.

"Enough to remove the cover over the well? Still, I can't believe anyone would deliberately leave a trap like that for any casual stranger to stumble into," Jim said.

"A trap?" Allegra's voice was higher than usual. "That's ridiculous."

A trap, Risa thought. A trap for me? She shook her head but hugged her arms to her body against the sudden chill that went through her.

7

The trip back to San Diego seemed to take forever. The fog wrapped them in a gray blanket, stifling their attempts at conversation. When at last the car began to climb the Ridge Route and they rose out of the Valley and its tule fog, Risa felt as though an actual weight had been lifted from her.

She glanced around at Allegra in the back and saw she had curled up on the seat, eyes closed. Despite the rummaging in a ruined house and a day of travel, Allegra looked uncrumpled, still pretty. Risa stared ruefully at her own disreputable clothes. She had washed her face and hands in the roadside café where they had eaten, but she knew she looked messy.

"You drove a long way for nothing," she said to Jim in a low voice.

"You found nothing?"

For a moment Risa thought he was asking again about the jar, not believing it had been empty. She touched the envelope in her coat pocket surreptitiously.

"No memories at all from the ranch?" Jim asked again, and she realized what he meant.

"Not from the —" she dropped her voice even lower and leaned toward Jim, "the lost year."

Jim flicked a glance at the rearview mirror.

"She's asleep," he said quietly. "I take it you haven't told Allegra about the memory loss."

"Ssh," Risa begged. "Please."

"She can't hear us," he said, but he lowered his voice. "Why don't you want her to know?"

"I don't trust her."

"Too pretty?"

She saw Jim was grinning. "What's that got to do with it?" Risa's voice rose and she forced herself to speak more softly. "Of course she's pretty. Rory wouldn't be interested in a girl that wasn't." And you wouldn't either, she added to herself. She began picking goatheads from her pant legs, though she knew the effort was wasted as far as appearance went — the pants were only fit for rags.

She was aware of Jim's frequent glances. "I know I look awful," she said finally. "You don't have to stare at me."

"Aren't those the same clothes you had on when I picked you up in the parking lot?"

"Yes."

"They're in bad shape."

"Well, I can't help it. I don't have any others. Beatrice gave all my clothes away when she thought I was — dead."

"And you haven't had time to buy any others?"

Risa looked down at her hands. "I don't have any money."

"Oh, come on. I saw five hundred dollars. Why not spend some of that?"

"I — I can't."

"Why not?"

"The man on the beach, the man with the beard. I was going to tell you but we went to Sharp Hospital and then I didn't want to spoil yesterday, and today you asked Allegra to come with us . . ."

"Wait — wait a minute. I didn't invite Allegra to go anywhere. When she appeared on the scene this morning I assumed you'd asked her along."

Risa stared at him. "But she — I . . ."

"All right. So she lied for some purpose of her own." He flicked another glance into the rear-view mirror. "That's over now. What about this man on the beach?"

"He had a knife and he called me by a wrong name and I was afraid, I didn't know him, he was a stranger, but he asked me for the money and I — I gave it to him."

Jim was silent a moment. "Do you think the man knew you?"

"I — don't know. I was frightened of him."

"What name did he call you?"

Risa searched her mind but the name was elusive. "I can't remember. Then there was a dog the night before. He followed me down to the beach and he knew me, I think, because he was so friendly. But I . . ." her words trailed away and she gazed despondently out through the windshield at the reddening sky. "Now I'm afraid to go to the beach, the house doesn't seem like mine anymore without Rory there, and she —" Risa jerked her head toward the back seat, "she's hiding Rory from me and I don't know what to do next."

"Do you want to go home, back to the house in Del Mar?"

Risa shook her head. "No. Only to see if Rory's there. If he's not I don't want to stay. It's like the house has changed, become unfriendly. I can't explain, but I don't belong at Del Mar now. Oh, Jim, what can I do?"

He was silent for so long that Risa gazed at him apprehensively. Would he tell her he couldn't help her any further? She was asking more and more of this man she had known for such a short while. Why should he spend so much of his time trying to unravel what might be an unsolvable problem?

"I can bring you to my apartment temporarily," he said, "if you feel you really can't stay at the Del Mar house."

"I — I — Thank you," she said. Any place was better than going back where Allegra was living. And surely he didn't mean, well, any actual involvement. He was merely offering her a place to stay. Wasn't he?

There was a noise from the back seat and Risa became aware of Allegra's presence once again. We've been talking in normal tones, she thought in dismay. If Allegra was awake she heard everything.

Allegra leaned over the front seat and yawned. "Aren't we nearly there?" she asked. "I can't stand much more of this cramped back seat."

"Twenty minutes," Jim said. He switched on the headlights.

There was no other car in front of the house when Jim came up the drive. Of course, Rory could have pulled the Ferrari — wait, would he have another Ferrari? — into the garage. Risa hurried into the house and sought out Beatrice.

"No Mister Rory hasn't called. Don't know when we're likely to see him. Seems as though Miss Allegra ought to know but she doesn't. I keep asking her." Beatrice shook her head. "You sure got dirty, Miss Risa."

Allegra stopped Risa as she neared the front door on her way back out of the house. "Where are you going?"

"Out."

Allegra's glance flicked up and down Risa. "I'd think you'd want to rest after your terrible experience today. And you certainly must feel grimy. Your clothes . . ." Allegra let the words fade away. "How long have you known Jim Halloway?" she asked.

"Awhile."

"I think he's an opportunist. Not that you aren't attractive. But haven't you wondered about his interest in you? After all, you haven't been at your best the last few days."

Risa laughed, a short clipped sound without humor. "So maybe I'm an interesting case to him. You know doctors."

"That's just it. I didn't want to hurt your feelings but I think you should ask yourself what his motives are."

Risa stared at Allegra. "What do you mean? I don't have any money, as you well know — Aunt Marie even left the ranch to Rory, not that it's worth much. And Jim probably has his choice of women. What other nefarious motives are there?"

"Your aunt didn't leave you anything at all?"

"Not a cent. She didn't have much, most of it came from Rory's father — like the house. She willed everything to Rory. Didn't he tell you?"

"He mentioned something of the sort but I wondered, since she was your aunt, not his. Well," Allegra shrugged, "don't say I didn't warn you."

Sour grapes. Annoyed because Jim didn't fall at her feet, Risa thought as she closed the front door behind her and headed for Jim's car. But a nagging uneasiness accompanied her to the Porsche, making her uncomfortable. They drove to San Diego in silence and her tension increased when Jim pulled into a parking slot behind a large apartment complex.

"Do — do you live here?" she asked as they got out of the car.

"Yes." He peered into her face. "What's the matter?"

"Nothing. I mean — I just wondered."

He had a ground-floor apartment, quite large and surprisingly bare. "I'm not here much," Jim said. "I keep thinking I'll buy a house sometime so

I haven't acquired more than the bare necessities."

Risa licked her lips and smiled politely.

"You look scared to death," he said. "A little lost waif."

She cleared her throat.

"The bathroom's in here," he said. "There's shampoo and all, towels in the cupboard."

She followed him and stood in the doorway. She could imagine filling the tub with hot water, climbing in and soaking away the dirt and frustration of the day. But . . .

Jim had disappeared, now he was back holding some garments out to her. "This is a scrub suit."

Risa took the green clothes from him and unfolded them. They were a short-sleeved slipover shirt and a pair of pants with a drawstring top. "A scrub suit?"

"Yes. Very glamorous. Sorry I can't do better but I didn't plan on you being here. Oh, the scrub suit. It's what I wear in surgery, the hospitals furnish them. I wore this one home once and never got around to returning it."

She turned the green cotton scrub suit over in her hands, not looking at him.

"It's clean — I wash clothes once a week. Honest."

"Yes, of course. Thank you." She knew the words were stilted and stiff.

He softly touched her shoulder. "Are you afraid of me, Risa? Is that what's wrong?"

She looked up at him and blinked as she tried to smile.

"Risa." He shook his head. "I didn't bring you here to take advantage of the situation. I hesitated a long time before I decided you might be better off away from Del Mar. There simply was no other place for you to go outside of a motel room somewhere and I felt you'd be afraid of staying alone at this point."

She nodded.

"You see —" he paused, smiled wryly, *"I'm* really afraid of *you.*"

"Of me? Why?"

"Because you *are* lost, you do need help, and you're a very appealing woman. I'm afraid of the combination. I was surprised and none too pleased to have Allegra come with us today, but in another way I was relieved. I don't have to worry about her, and her presence prevented us from being alone."

"I — I thought you admired her."

"What man wouldn't? She's very pretty. But attracted to her?" Jim shook his head. "Not more than a surface attraction."

"I don't understand what you mean about being afraid," Risa said.

"Risa — what do you think about me?"

"You're kind, you've spent a great deal of your time trying to help me, gone out of your way . . ."

"And you've wondered why."

"Well . . ." She turned away from him, turned back. "Well, yes I have." Allegra's voice rang in her ears. What are his motives?

"I have a friend who's a psychiatrist," Jim said.

"He's tried to teach me to examine my feelings, pick them apart instead of allowing them to hide possible truths from me. And the truth of it is, I'm afraid I'm attracted to you because you remind me of my wife."

Risa stood stunned, unable to react at all.

"She had problems I thought I was going to solve. I thought when we married I could make everything different for her." Jim shook his head.

"What happened?" Risa managed to ask.

"The fifth time she tried to kill herself she succeeded. I've never believed she wanted to die that time, it was only another attempt to control my actions. But she misjudged." Jim's voice faltered and Risa saw he had trouble speaking. "I didn't take her call. I was busy at the hospital, they told me about the phone call, she was always calling with demands and threats and I put it out of my mind and stayed on at the hospital until I was finished there. When I got home she was dead, she'd taken enough barbiturates to kill several people."

"I'm — sorry," Risa said. "But are you saying you think I'm like her? Do you mean you're afraid I would — that I want to die?"

"No, not that at all. My reactions to you are what bother me. Am I making the same mistake I made before? My psychiatrist friend showed me how my own needs attracted me to Mary and at the same time blinded me to the fact I was making her worse. She needed a different kind of attention than a husband's. She needed a psychiatrist. She was beyond the reach of love and kindness by the time I knew her. I should have seen it, I was interning by then, I had enough medical knowledge. But she was frail and appealing, a little girl lost."

Risa pushed her hands out as though thrusting the words from her.

"So I think I should find professional help for you now, rather than make a mistake, let the situation get out of hand. I should have insisted on it from the beginning. Now wait — don't get upset. The psychiatrist I've been talking about is a very fine doctor as well as my friend."

"No," Risa breathed.

"Listen to me. I'll talk to him first, he'll see you in an informal way. Maybe he'll let me be with you the first time."

"You think I'm out of my mind," Risa said.

Jim sighed. "No. I don't. But you need help, you've asked me to help you and this is the best help I can provide. You'll like Mac, he won't scare you. He may be able to lead you into enough memory recall so your lost year will belong to you again."

Risa picked three goatheads from her pants and rolled the prickly seeds in her fingers. The tiny prongs jabbed her skin, hurting her. He'll hurt me too, the psychiatrist, she thought. He'll poke into my mind and I don't know what he'll find. I'm afraid.

❧ 8 ❧

Risa stared at Jim hopelessly. He turned his head away.

"Go take your bath," he said.

Risa almost fell asleep in the tub. When she got out she toweled her hair until it curled damply over her head and climbed into Jim's green scrub suit. She had to roll up the pant legs and the shirt ended at her knees but she felt clean all the way through; she felt better. Almost confident enough to accept the idea of a psychiatrist.

Jim was waiting for her in the living room. He had her car coat in one hand and the envelope in the other.

"This came out of the jar, didn't it?" he asked, narrowing his eyes as he watched her.

Risa stiffened. "Are you getting a habit of going through my pockets?"

"I picked up the coat and this fell out." He thrust the envelope at her. "I've known all along the jar wasn't empty. Don't you trust anyone?"

Yes, she thought, I trust Rory. But I can't find him. She looked at Jim and saw the disappointment in his face.

"I — I don't know why I didn't tell you," she said. "I guess I was afraid Allegra . . ."

"How many other things are you concealing either by omission or commission?" he demanded. "What good does it do to ask for help and then lie to me?"

She twisted her hands together and looked away from him. "I haven't lied," she said.

"You did about the jar." Jim's voice betrayed his anger. "Is this some kind of game you're playing — the frightened waif act, the lost year? I'm beginning to believe Allegra. She said you were devious."

"But she doesn't know me," Risa cried. "She's trying to turn you against me, me against you, and I have no idea why."

"You're doing a pretty good job of it on your own," Jim said. "I don't know how much of your story I believe now."

She stared up at him. His eyes seemed darker, opaque, closed against her. Her shoulders drooped.

"Well," he demanded, "aren't you going to take this?"

Risa realized he was still holding the envelope. She swallowed in an effort to gain control of her voice. He would think tears were part of an act. "Can't we open it together?" she asked, her voice husky with the unshed tears.

Without a word Jim moved to the couch, sat down. She hesitated, then came to sit tentatively beside him. He handed her the envelope and she made a gesture of refusal. "No, you open it. Please."

He tore the envelope carefully, methodically, opening it across the top, then with a sudden move, spilled the contents in her lap. Folded papers, a photograph.

Risa picked up the passport-sized picture. A dark young man, unsmiling, head and shoulders only. A stranger. She handed the photograph to Jim. He examined the man, looked at her.

"Similar bone structure," he said.

"What?"

"You resemble this man." He turned the picture over.

"My love forever," he read, "until death do us part. Tony."

"My — my father?"

"Could be."

She stared at the photograph in wonderment.

"What else is there?" Jim asked.

Risa unfolded a paper. "My dearest Merry . . . "

"This is written to my mother," she said to Jim. "Her name was Meredith. Meredith and Marie, the MacArthur Sisters."

"What?"

"They used to travel around California, making a living with violin concerts." Risa was conscious of delaying the moment she would have to read the letter. Though she longed to know the contents, she had a sense of violation.

"My dearest Merry . . ." she began again, "I'm glad she was born in November, it's a lucky month for your family, like you told me. And the name, Risa Antonia, just as I asked. You know why I can't come to you, I've told you of the danger to you and to the baby.

"We could meet if you're able to leave Risa with someone. Come to the same place as before, on a Saturday. I'll look for you and pray you'll be there. Don't worry about Risa, she'll be taken care of. My love forever, Tony."

Risa closed her eyes. "I can't read the next one."

"Do you want me to?"

"Please."

A rustle of paper and then she heard Jim's quiet voice:

"A topaz for my Lady Fair,
November born so she may wear
The golden sun within this stone,
An amulet for her alone
To keep her safe from violent harm
And bring her love and gentle charm."

Risa's eyes flew open. She brought her legs up under her on the couch, leaned over to look at what Jim was reading. He handed her a yellowed paper written on in flowing script, the ink faded to brown. The handwriting was elegant in an old-fashioned manner.

"Tony didn't write this," she said.

"No," Jim agreed, "it's much older."

"A topaz for my Lady Fair . . ." Jim repeated. "That might be you."

"But the poem was written long ago." Risa looked up from the lines and into Jim's eyes. The gold flecks were back. She couldn't look away.

88

Her breath seemed to catch in her throat, time had stopped, there was nothing else but the two of them, Jim and Risa.

His fingers touched her face, her neck. "You're the lady of the poem, all the same," he said. "A lovely lost lady."

Lost, she thought, the word echoing unpleasantly in her mind, breaking the spell of Jim's voice, his touch. She pulled away.

"Let's read the rest of these," she said.

There were two more letters. One was from Tony to her mother, seemingly written in a hurry for the writing was scrawled across the page. "Give the enclosed to your sister . . ." Risa read, "and leave the baby with her. Meet me as soon as you can. We have to leave this week or there won't be another chance." There was no indication what the enclosed had been, and the other letter was different altogether.

"Dear Meredith . . ." it said. "The brooch must be entrusted to you as Marie has too often indicated her unwillingness to follow family tradition. As you know, it can only be worn by a female descendent born in November. Therefore, the topaz has not been worn for two generations now, but I trust you will be fortunate enough to have a November-born girl when you marry. Marie is a spinster to the bone and I cannot believe she will change in this or any other respect. She is my own granddaughter but she lacks warmth. As the elder girl, I should entrust her to hand down the stone but I refuse to do so for the reasons I have given.

"With the topaz brooch is the original verse written by your great-grandfather when he presented the gem to your great-grandmother as her wedding gift. The topaz itself had been in his family for many generations, but he had it set into the brooch for his November-born bride. Give the verse and the topaz brooch to your daughter (for you will have one someday, I have the feeling, my Scots blood letting me see ahead) when she is old enough to know she has been chosen. My love to you. Rowan Cameron Wallace."

"The topaz," Risa said softly. "My topaz."

"Where is it now?" Jim's question shattered the warm cocoon that had enveloped Risa as she read the letter.

"I don't know." She grasped his arm. "Oh, Jim, I must find the topaz again."

"When did your mother give it to you?"

"I — she didn't. I told you my aunt raised me. I didn't even know about the topaz, that it belonged in the family, that I was to have it."

"Then who *gave* you the brooch, when did you get it?"

Risa stared blankly at Jim. "I can't remember."

"The memory probably belongs with the other missing events of the past year. Somehow you acquired the topaz during that time."

"And lost it again." Risa's voice was sad.

"Your aunt didn't . . . ?"

"She died a few weeks before I went to Baja

with Rory. She never mentioned a topaz brooch."

"Did Rory?"

Her eyes widened in surprise. "He wouldn't know anything about it. He's not part of my family, not really."

"Yet you seem closely attached to him." Jim's voice had a slight edge.

"Well, he's almost like a brother."

"Is that how you feel about him?"

No, Risa thought unhappily. I love him. I want to be with him all the time, forever. And not have Allegra exist.

"And does he think of you as his little sister?"

"I don't know. I suppose he does." Oh, Rory, she cried to herself. Why aren't you here to comfort me?

"What will he do when he comes back and finds you miraculously alive, with an unknown girl buried by mistake in your grave?"

"He'll straighten everything out," she said. "He'll discover why I can't remember, he'll find out what happened."

"How?"

"I don't know — but he will, he will."

"Then all you want from me is a place to stay until you locate this superman."

They glared at one another. "I can stay in my own house," she cried.

"But you didn't want to."

Risa buried her face in her hands. "Oh, why can't it be last November again?" She felt Jim's hand on her hair.

"I'm sorry," he said. "Why don't you go to bed? You can have the bedroom; I'll sleep on the couch, and I'll see you in the morning."

Risa went into the bedroom. Jim had changed the sheets on the bed, left the covers turned down for her. She thought of his fingers along her face, the moment when he might have kissed her. Does he really think I'm pretty? she wondered. A lady fair? Not merely someone with problems, someone like his dead wife?

She snuggled under the blanket. I'm safe, she told herself. No one knows where I am except Jim. Allegra may suspect, but Jim's phone number isn't listed so she can't look up his address. The man with the beard can't find me. No one can.

She closed her eyes. I wonder if my mother was able to meet Tony? she thought. Where did they go? Aunt Marie told me they were dead, they died together but she didn't tell me how. It's hard to say "my father." He's always been Tony in my mind, I used to chant the name over and over to put myself to sleep when I was little. I never had anything else of my father but his first name. Now I have the two letters he wrote my mother. "My dearest Merry . . ."

"She was a sweet girl but too suggestible," Aunt Marie used to say of Risa's mother. "She could be talked into things that were bad for her, wrong." Aunt Marie had insisted Risa could have no recollection of her mother because she was so small when her mother left her there at the ranch, left her for good. But I remember frag-

92

ments, Risa thought. Aunt Marie called them dreams and maybe they were. The feeling someone called her name over and over, telling her to come. I followed the dreams and walked in my sleep to the sycamore grove, Risa said to herself. I awoke there time and again thinking she had left something for me. And she had, she'd left the jar, surely it was my mother who put the papers in the jar and hid it in the old well. Jim had found the jar today, given Risa a bit of both her mother and father and the beautiful poem to go with the topaz brooch. Jim had saved her life.

She saw the twisted prongs of the hay fork in her mind and turned on her side, curling into a ball. I won't think about falling, she said to herself, about falling and dying . . .

Jim had given her the verse but the topaz was missing. If she had it now, held close in her hand, warm and golden, nothing could harm her ever again. An amulet, her amulet. But gone. Missing with the past year.

What could she do to search for what she had lost? A psychiatrist, Jim said. Trust me, Jim said.

Risa woke to a room filled with sunlight. Through the door she could hear movement, sounds. She got out of bed and went into the bathroom, where she stared at her flushed face and tousled dark curls in the mirror over the sink. The dark circles were gone, her eyes were clear. I look better, she told herself. I feel better. I'll see Jim's friend, there's no reason to fear a psychiatrist.

❧ 9 ❧

She found Jim in the kitchen scrambling eggs. "Good morning," she said. "Are those for me?"

"For us. My one talent — knowing how eggs should be scrambled. Why don't you put some bread in the toaster, I've got to stop at the hospital before I go to the office and it's getting late."

Jim hurried through breakfast and she left her unfinished plate to walk to the door with him.

"We'll have to decide what to do with you," he said. "But for now I want you to go shopping. Buy some clothes for yourself, you can't live in those torn brown pants forever."

Risa glanced at the rumpled green scrub suit, thought of her only other clothes in the bedroom. "You know I don't have any money."

"I'm lending you some." He handed her four twenties. Risa took the bills hesitantly, knowing she had to have other clothes to wear but concerned about taking money she wasn't sure she could pay back.

"I don't know when I can repay you but . . ."

"I'm not worrying," he said. He leaned toward her, then pulled back.

I wonder if he was going to kiss me good-bye? she thought. Maybe like he did his wife. Risa moved out of reach. I'm not Mary, not his wife, not like her at all, she told herself indignantly.

"I won't be home before six-thirty, maybe seven," he said. "And I'm on call tonight, so I might be even later. But I'll be here."

Risa nodded, closed the door after him, and went back to her breakfast. After she ate she cleaned the kitchen, straightened the apartment. Jim is so neat, she said to herself. Not at all like Rory, who strews his belongings all over the house, expecting everyone else to do his picking up. Rory. Was he home?

She went to the telephone and called the house at Del Mar. There was no answer.

When she arrived at the shopping center, Risa felt an irrational excitement, the elation of a child picking out her own presents. At a sale she found a rust-colored pantsuit that fit her beautifully. She bought new shoes, underclothes and cosmetics, debated over pajamas and then decided to save the change from the last twenty for incidental expenses. I can always wear the scrub suit for pajamas, she told herself.

Back at the apartment, the time dragged without Jim there. Risa picked up magazines but found them mostly medical — *The New England Journal of Medicine, Medical Digest* . . . She turned on the TV and found she didn't care for the day-time programs, which she had never watched. She thought of starting to fix an evening meal but rejected the idea because she wasn't sure when Jim would be home.

I wish he had a piano, she thought. If I was home I could sit down and . . . Then she remembered there was no longer a piano at Del Mar. Did Rory sell it? she wondered again.

When Jim finally arrived at the apartment it was after eight. Risa was curled on the couch asleep. She sat up when she heard his key in the lock.

"Well," he said as he surveyed her from head to foot, "quite an improvement."

"Thank you," she said, suddenly shy.

"I thought we'd eat out," he said. "I'll have to bring the beeper along." He indicated a small black box hooked to his belt. "I'm still on call."

"I would have gotten supper," she said, "but I didn't know when to plan it for."

At the restaurant, he again examined her. This time across the table. "You do look different. Less strained."

"I slept well last night. That helped."

"No dreams?"

Risa hesitated. "I think I — yes, I did have my dream about the topaz, about standing on the rocks above the ocean and holding the topaz, frightened because — because — well, I don't know why, but in the dream I was."

"Could the rocks be real, could you have dreamed about somewhere you've been? Like Baja, for instance?"

"No." Risa blurted the word, then paused. "I don't know why I disagreed so fast. There's no reason the ocean and the rocks couldn't be. The desolate landscape in my dream is like Baja. Barren."

"Have you considered that maybe Rory gave

you the topaz brooch on your trip to Mexico and you're remembering it in a dream fragment?"

"But he couldn't have given me the brooch. It wasn't his."

"Who went through your aunt's belongings after she died?"

"We both did, Rory and I."

Jim shrugged his shoulders. "It's not impossible then."

Risa shook her head, unconvinced.

"I'm off Wednesday afternoon," Jim said. "Maybe we should drive down to Baja and see if any specific locale triggers memories for you."

"I thought you were going to have your psychiatrist friend find my memories for me."

"Don't fight the idea, Risa. Mac is a capable doctor. But better than that, he's a nice guy. You'll like him."

Risa took a deep breath and twisted her hands together. What was in her mind that she could not reach and a stranger might be able to? "When do I have to see him?" she asked.

"He said he had time to drop by the apartment around nine-thirty. Sort of a get-acquainted visit, maybe a few preliminary questions so he can begin to know you."

Risa shivered. "I'm still afraid," she said.

"Mac straightened me out during a bad time," Jim said. "I told you last night about Mary. She's been dead three years and only in the past year have I been free of guilt. I know now I couldn't have cured her by anything I personally did or didn't do. But I'd never have seen my way out except for Mac. There's nothing frightening about a psychiatrist. Mac's only a person who's a little better equipped than the rest of us to see what's happening inside a head."

"That's what scares me — he'll see things I don't know are there, in my head," Risa said.

"What you would remember are your own memories, and knowing is better than wondering the rest of your life."

"I might be better off not knowing," she said. "How can I ever tell?"

"I'd like to know one thing myself," Jim said. He reached over the table and touched Risa's hand. "What other man is in your life, in your lost year?"

Risa shook her head. Surely she wouldn't forget someone she loved, and anyway, Rory was more important than any mythical man. "I called Del Mar," she said. "No one was home. If Rory doesn't get back soon I don't know what I should do. I mean, I'm not really dead. Isn't there something I ought to do about letting someone know? Maybe the police?"

"I have no idea, Risa, I'll have to find out. If you had a will it's probably gone through probate by now. I imagine the court would have to be told you're alive."

"I did make out a will after Aunt Marie died — but I didn't have anything to leave to Rory, not really."

"What prompted you to make a will?"

"Well, Rory made his will out in favor of me so

I made mine to him. He wanted me to have the house and anything else he had in case something happened to him. He said we weren't blood relatives so he had to make sure. Oh, Jim, do you think something *has* happened to him?"

"No. Allegra would certainly know. Why would she conceal it from you?"

"But she does lie, she lied to me about you asking her to drive to the ranch. I don't trust her, I think she knows where Rory is and won't tell him I'm alive."

Jim shrugged. "I can't understand what motive she'd have."

"Maybe they're not really engaged, maybe . . ."

"What does your housekeeper say?"

Risa sighed. "She says they are. She says Rory brought Allegra to the house."

"Well. That makes your theory pretty shaky."

"I know something is wrong, Jim, I can feel the wrongness. I just can't find what it is."

Jim's beeper sounded, he flicked the switch and stood up. "I'll have to call in," he said.

When he came back from phoning, he seemed distracted and they finished their meal without further conversation and left the restaurant.

"I hope I won't have to go out before Mac gets to the apartment," Jim said. "I took care of that call over the phone, but there are some you can't."

The apartment was beginning to be familiar enough to Risa so she felt at home. "I wish you had a piano," she told Jim. "I miss not playing."

"You're a musician?"

"Oh, not for anyone's amusement but my own. Aunt Marie used to tell me I was lazy, playing as well as I did and not doing any more about it. But I'm not a concert pianist. Actually, I'd rather fool around with the popular stuff, I have more fun with it."

"I'd like to hear you play."

Risa smiled. "Sometime I'll take you up on that," she said. "You'll be sorry."

They were both still standing, though Jim had closed the door. He was near enough to touch her although he hadn't. Risa felt a growing awareness of him, which became so strong she couldn't meet his eyes.

"What's the matter?" he asked, stepping closer and placing his hands on her arms. She shivered.

"Look at me," Jim demanded.

Risa brought her eyes up to his. The yellow flecks in his irises glowed. She tried to smile, tried to say something, anything, but all she could do was look at him.

"Risa, we have to learn about your lost time fast. We must know or else forget about that year altogether and pretend it didn't occur. One or the other. We can't wait suspended here."

She wanted him to hold her close, she could feel her veins throbbing with a new urgency. His hands slid down her arms, pulled her to him.

The doorbell rang.

Risa moved out of Jim's arms, disappointed, feeling a sense of loss but at the same time relieved that no commitment had to be made. She walked into the living room and sat on the couch, took a deep breath and hugged herself, keeping her arms crossed over her chest.

Dr. Howard McInerney was taller than Jim, thinner. He wore his hair long, and his beard and mustache merged so Risa felt all she could really see of him were his eyes, bright blue and watchful.

"This is Mac," Jim said. They came into the living room. Jim sat on the couch with her, Mac on the nearest chair.

"Your name is interesting, Risa. I'm sure you've been told the meaning."

"Yes — laughter." She glanced at Jim. "He doesn't think it fits me." The words came out in a rush, nervously.

Jim reached over and squeezed her hand. Risa glanced at Mac and knew he had seen the gesture, filed it away for reference.

"I'm sure your name was well chosen. Problems keep us all from laughter some time or another, but problems can be dealt with. Jim tells me your present problem is amnesia. All the word means, you know, is forgetting selected events."

"But I didn't want to forget anything," she cried.

Mac smiled ruefully. "Amnesia isn't a lapse of memory exactly. Medically we call it dissociation — you know how doctors like to complicate things with labels. What dissociation means is a splitting off of a group of memories too painful to be retained."

"What could these be?" she asked.

"Only your unconscious mind knows," he said. "Whatever it was upset you to the extent that you pushed the memory into an area of your mind where you can't reach it right now."

"A whole year of memories?"

"The time can vary. Amnesia can affect your sense of who you are or when you are."

"I know who I am."

"You know who you are today," Mac said. "But perhaps not who you were a month ago. Will you try a few exercises with me to search for a locked cubbyhole somewhere in your mind? I don't propose to do anything frightening. In fact if we do touch on a taboo area we'll stop immediately. I don't expect to learn much tonight, but neither do I expect to disturb and upset you. We'll regard this as preliminary only."

"What — what are you going to do?"

"Nothing, unless you want me to. Nothing that frightens you."

"Is it — would it be like hypnosis?"

"You've been a sleepwalker in the past, right?" When Risa nodded he went on. "Then you can remember how you felt, how you seemed to be awake and yet weren't. Was it frightening to you?"

"No. Except I'd wake up outside sometimes. I was a child then and I wouldn't know why I wasn't in the house, and it was night and I was scared."

"Okay. Now I'll talk to you. After a while you

may feel you are here with Jim and me in the room and yet not quite. It's like sleepwalking, only we'll make sure you don't wander away."

"Look inside your head," Mac told her. "Concentrate on a point behind your forehead. Close your eyes if that makes it easier to do. Think of the point you've chosen, otherwise let your mind drift, don't think of anything else." His voice went on and on, monotonous, saying the same thing over and over in different ways, and Risa relaxed, listening, only half listening, then hearing the low even voice without really listening at all.

Images swirled through her mind. She had started for Baja, she and Rory. Had the voice told her or was she remembering? But it didn't matter, Rory sat beside her, twisting the wheel of the Ferrari expertly as they traveled around the curves to Ensenada. Rory was with her and everything was as it had been, everything was all right.

A sense of discomfort grew in her chest until she couldn't breathe. If she turned her head she would see Rory beside her, of course it was Rory driving the copper Ferrari, she wouldn't bother to look, but she had to see, she had to turn her head. Suddenly she felt the steering wheel under her own hands and when she turned to see who rode with her she saw a stranger, blood pouring from her face, blood on the white T-shirt, trickling over the brooch pinned to the shirt. The topaz brooch. Risa screamed.

❧ 10 ❧

Risa could hear screams. Her own? Arms caught at her, tried to hold her, she fought and a voice said, "No, let her go, Jim, she's too upset to know you," and the arms dropped away.

She opened her eyes and found she was standing in a room with two men. For an instant everything was strange, wrong, and then she recognized Jim. Jim, yes, and the other man was his friend, Mac — was the psychiatrist. Risa shrank against Jim and he put his arm around her.

Mac did not move at all. "I'm sorry you were frightened, Risa," he said. "Evidently what you fear is very close to the surface. We won't try this method again soon." He smiled at her, nodded to Jim, and went out the door.

"Do you want to talk about it?" Jim asked, leading her to the couch and making her sit down.

She shook her head. "It was something about the trip to Baja, something awful. I don't want to think about . . ." She covered her face with her hands and began to sob.

Jim gathered her close, held her until she stopped crying.

"Do you think you can sleep?" he asked.

She shook her head again, ashamed to admit

what she really feared was being alone in the bedroom.

"I'll get you something to help." He touched her still wet cheek. "Go wash your face."

Risa avoided her eyes in the mirror, afraid she might see another Risa, one who knew what the scene in her mind a few minutes ago had meant.

She swallowed the capsule Jim gave her.

"In the morning you'll feel better," he said. "Sleep helps."

Despite the medication, she had trouble falling asleep. At first she lay rigid in bed, willing her eyes to open to keep from seeing images behind her closed lids. Then when the capsule began to overcome her she fought in vain against the downward swirling, the sense of heaviness . . .

She woke in the morning with Jim touching her shoulder, speaking her name. He stood beside the bed, fully dressed.

"I'm leaving in a few minutes," he said. "I didn't like to go without telling you."

Risa struggled to sit up. She had a dull ache in her temples and her movements seemed sluggish.

"How are you?" Jim asked.

"Um — all right, I guess. Still half asleep."

"I made some coffee."

"Thanks."

"Risa . . ." He sat down on the bed. "I want you to see Mac again. In his office, in a regular therapy session. Will you?"

Unwillingness clouded her mind. She shook her head.

"I think you should. Will you do it for me? Try it one more time?"

Risa looked into Jim's eyes, saw the tenderness and concern. Slowly she nodded, although she felt her stomach contract in disagreement.

"Mac was very upset about what happened last night and worried about leaving you with the unpleasant experience still in your mind."

"I — he — I suppose it wasn't his fault."

"He thinks it was, blames himself for moving too fast. He called to tell me he has a cancellation this afternoon and could see you then if you're willing to come."

So soon, she thought. I can't. But Jim bent over and touched her lips lightly with his.

"One o'clock," he said. "I'll pick you up right after twelve."

When Jim had left, Risa got up, showered and dressed in the rust pantsuit. Moving like an automaton, she fixed toast and ate breakfast without tasting the food at all. She tidied up the apartment, turned on the TV and sat in front of it watching and yet not following the programs. She still had a heavy feeling and dropped off to sleep several times. At noon the phone rang.

"Risa, I won't be able to get away," Jim said. "I'm at the hospital. Have you got any money left?"

"Yes."

"You can take a cab to Mac's office. Or a bus if you don't have enough for the cab."

"I'll take a bus," she said with no thought in

her mind except the bus would take longer to get there.

"There's a bus that'll take you downtown. The bus stop is on the corner — there's a sign." He gave her Mac's address, which was in the downtown area.

"All right," she said.

"Risa."

"Yes?"

"You are going to go, aren't you?"

"I said I would." She knew her voice was sullen but she felt Jim had coerced her into going, she didn't want to ever see Howard McInerney again.

The bus came far too quickly and by twelve thirty-five she was downtown, ready to walk the several blocks to Mac's office. She slowed her pace, glancing into store windows, stopping when she saw something interesting. But inexorably she moved closer to Mac.

"Hello there, Topaz," a voice said.

The word made her turn. To her surprise, a middle-aged man, beginning to go bald, stood beside her, looking directly at her.

"We've really missed you," he said. "I heard you were sick."

He was talking to her, there was no mistake. What could he mean?

Confused, she shook her head, unable to think of what to say.

"Well, glad to see you're better, hope you'll be

back next weekend."

He waved a hand and rejoined the crowd on the sidewalk, moving away from her.

Risa stared after him, then turned to walk the last block to the psychiatrist's office. She took two steps and stopped. Topaz, she thought in confusion, he called me Topaz. And the man on the beach, the man with the beard called me another name too. Not Topaz, I would have remembered. But another name, not Risa. Did both the men make a mistake or am I someone else, even two other people?

Without warning the image of Rory driving the Ferrari with her in the passenger seat flashed into her mind. No, she thought, I don't want to see the rest, I can't . . .

She turned and began walking rapidly, half running, away from the address Jim had given her, moving without thinking, without a destination in mind. But away from Mac.

She came to the Plaza, where the city buses picked up and unloaded. I don't want to go back to Jim's apartment, she thought. Or to Del Mar. She saw the Greyhound depot down the street and then she knew where she was going to go. To Ensenada, to the source of the rocks and the topaz.

Inside the bus station she called Del Mar and got Allegra.

"No, Rory hasn't called," Allegra told her. "But where are you, in case he does?"

"I — I'm going to Baja, to Ensenada," Risa

said. "I'll call when I get back."

Once on the bus to Mexico, Risa had second thoughts. How was she ever going to explain running away to Jim? It wasn't his fault, wasn't really Mac's fault either. She had been so afraid, no use to think about it. She would try to remember where the rocks had been instead. Maybe if she went to the beach, walked along the sand, she would find the dream landscape and know when she'd been there. Maybe she could even find Rory. He could be fishing, she would look for the boat while she was in Ensenada. Maybe he was there.

Risa sat next to a window as the bus left Tijuana. When the road neared the coast, she began watching for the islands Rory always had her spot. Islas Los Coronados, the Coronado Islands.

"Good fishing there if you can outwit the Mex patrol boats," he would say. And when she protested, "Oh, sure I can get the damn license but why bother? Takes all the fun out of it."

The shoreline rose in low bluffs above the ocean, rising and falling in a series of barren rock vistas. The Pacific sparkled blue and green in the sun. Beauty, but of a starkness she found unnerving.

MEDAÑOS, a road sign read. Sand dunes. Dune buggies raced and skidded up and down the dunes, their colors garish against the bleak landscape. Soon they would be at Punta Salsipuedes. Get-Out-If-You-Can Point. She had laughed the first time it was translated for her. That was before she had seen the handwrought iron cross on the rocky tip, dedicated to the souls of those who did not get out.

Past the point was Bahía Salsipuedes, the bay, and when the bus stopped to pick up a shawl-wrapped Mexican woman, Risa obeyed a sudden impulse and got off. She had been on the beach here before with Rory. She would go again now. But when the bus pulled away she looked after it, disturbed by being alone.

She left the road and headed for the beach, climbing over and around rocks and finally picking her way gingerly down the bluff. About halfway down she saw she had made a bad choice and would have to climb back up to the top and choose a new descent. She rested for a bit on the rocky overhang, watching gulls swoop above the water and cluster in the air above a fishing boat making its way south.

There was no way down from the ledge, though she could, of course, go up. But she felt a certain perverse satisfaction in remaining where she was. Here am I, she thought, stranded in Baja by my own foolishness. I could have waited until Wednesday and come with Jim. Why did I ran? What frightened me was in my own head, not Mac's. He didn't make me see anything, he merely gave me the chance to look.

What if I imagined a dead girl? she asked herself. After all, someone did die and was buried in my place. Maybe I created a horrible fantasy figure to put in the Ferrari and I've been scared by my own imagination. But beneath her rationalizing she knew she did not want to look at anything like the bloody figure in Rory's car again.

I can't stay here, she thought. It's getting on in the afternoon and I'm certainly several miles from anyplace to eat or to spend the night. Or to get a bus back, for that matter. Why didn't I go on down to Ensenada in the first place?

Because the rocks are here. The words were in her head as though someone had said them aloud. The rocks are here. She peered over the ledge at the steep drop below her. Not this rock, not this ledge, she thought. I've never been here before. She pulled herself upward, climbing to the top of the bluff, where she walked along heading south, searching for a better way down to the beach.

She came to a dip where an arroyo cut through the rocks to the sea. Cautiously, careful of footholds, she began to descend once again, taking her time to choose the best path. I'm near that old shipwreck, she thought. It was just south of here where Rory took me to see the wreck. Did we go last November to see it again? No, because he was in a hurry, we wouldn't have stopped.

You don't remember, the voice in her head whispered. You remember the rocks and the topaz and nothing else. And the rocks are here.

At last she was at the base of the bluff, where the ocean lapped at a pebbled beach. She skirted the cliff, heading for the mouth of the arroyo, where sand formed a wide barrier between rock and water. There was no one on the beach except Risa and the shore birds. She looked up at the bluff. Had someone moved? But though she stared for a long time, she saw nothing.

But now she felt exposed on the open beach and she retraced her steps, intending to climb back to the highway and walk toward Ensenada. San Miguel wasn't far and she knew there would be food there, possibly someone heading on to Ensenada.

The sun was setting into low clouds along the horizon and the sky flamed. Shadows sprang into place between the rocks as Risa began the upward climb. A pulsing throbbed at her left temple and her skin pricked with apprehension. "Nothing's wrong," she whispered to herself, but the hair on the back of her neck rose and she shivered. She stopped, looked above her, but the rocks blocked her view. She resumed climbing when suddenly a small stone clattered past her and went bouncing down the cliff. She froze.

There was no way she could have dislodged the stone — it had come from above. She tried to project a mental picture of a ground squirrel running over the rocks, pushing a stone out of place, but the image refused to form. Someone was up there.

❧ *11* ❧

Risa crouched in the shadows between the rocks. The fingers of her right hand curled over the palm and she realized she was fondling a topaz that was not there. The topaz brooch should be with me now, she thought. I had it the other time, when I climbed down and got to the beach. My head hurt but I had the topaz . . .

Her thought broke off. What other time? she asked herself, all the time straining her ears to hear any sound that would betray the one above her. She shook her head, tried to tell herself she was being silly, no one was there, she should climb to the top and head for San Miguel before dark. Her body refused to obey, hunching against the rock, hiding in the deepest of the shadows.

Then at last there came a sound, movement above and to her right. Slight scuffling noises as of shoes on rock. Closer. She held her breath.

"Risa." A soft sibilant, a whisper, sexless.

Despite herself she gave a small whimper of fright.

Something brushed her arm and she jerked away, fell sideways into space. She opened her mouth to scream but the sound didn't get out before she slammed into a rock, knocking the breath from her. She lay stunned, listening to stones rattle down the slope beneath her.

Then there was a silence. Slowly she pulled herself to her knees, then got her feet underneath her, but remained crouching between the rock and the bluff in the depression that had stopped her fall. Her left knee hurt but she could move it.

Who knew she was here? She had said Ensenada to Allegra on the phone but this wasn't — she had never gotten to Ensenada. And yet the voice had whispered her name. He's been waiting, she thought, waiting for me to come back, knowing I would have to, I'd be drawn to this spot. But who is it? The man with the beard? He hadn't called her Risa . . .

Movement to her right again, so stealthy she sensed rather than heard or saw it. Was it like this the time before when she held the topaz? With her trapped and desperate waiting for the un-known pursuer to discover her hiding place? Risa couldn't remember.

Why would anyone want her to die? The cover removed from the well at the ranch — had that been a trap for her? What had she done that would make anybody want to kill her? It had to be in the lost year.

A small avalanche of stones slid past her, more scrabbling of feet. She cringed away from the sound.

"Risa!" A loud call this time. "Is that you down there? Risa?" Was it the same voice?

There was a sudden scrambling to her right and someone went past her, up the cliff, climbing fast, a dark figure, she could see no details in the dusk. After a moment a car started, roared away.

"Risa," the call came again.

Jim? She pulled herself from her hiding place and answered. "I'm here."

Shoes on the rocks and a dark figure above her.

"Jim?" she asked.

"Oh, for God's sake, Risa, yes, it's Jim."

He grabbed her arm, helped her the rest of the way up the slope. At the top she clung to him.

"There was someone else," she said. "I don't know who."

"He drives a gold sports car," Jim said grimly. "I couldn't see the make. Didn't see much of him either. I wasn't expecting anyone to rush by me like that."

"He was after me, I know he was."

"Are you all right?"

"Yes, I hurt my knee a little but I'm okay. Do you think he could have been the man with the beard?"

"I don't know," Jim said. He held her away from him. "What in hell persuaded you to run off to Baja on your own? Mac called me to say you'd missed your appointment and I knew something was wrong."

"How — how did you know where to find me?"

"I called Allegra. She tried to play dumb but I told her she either told me or I called the police." Jim shrugged. "That seemed to scare her for some reason."

"The police?" Risa said.

"How did I know what had happened to you? But she said you'd called and so I drove down to Ensenada to check out all the buses coming in, and the driver of yours remembered you getting off in the middle of nowhere." It was too dark to see Jim's expression.

"I — It was an impulse, but I was right, this is the place, the place where I had the topaz. Some of the memory came back about climbing down to the beach, but the man was stalking me and I couldn't remember any more." She gripped Jim's arm. "But don't you see? I was here, this is the place. How did I know to get off the bus exactly here?"

"We can talk on the way back," Jim said.

"Oh, no, I want to stay, come to these rocks again tomorrow when it's light. Please come with me, I'm afraid to be alone here now. Oh . . ." Her words trailed off. "I'm sorry. I keep forgetting you have to work."

Jim was quiet a moment. "I'm off in the afternoon anyway," he said finally. "I suppose I can take the morning too. We'll go down to Ensenada to eat and I'll call San Diego and see what I can arrange."

The El Rey Sol Restaurant was happy to serve the señor and provide a place for the señorita to wash herself and brush her clothes.

"I've ordered you a marguerita," Jim said when she came back to the table.

116

Risa nodded, looked around the restaurant. Had she ever been here before? It seemed almost familiar but she couldn't be sure. She sipped her drink, licked the salt from her lips.

"How's your knee?"

"A lot better since you wrapped the elastic bandage around it."

"Good. Now tell me why you ran away? Mac is climbing the walls, blaming himself for unprofessional conduct, and is mad at me for talking him into that informal session to begin with. So — what happened?"

Risa shook her head. "Nothing. I didn't want to go to see Mac, I was afraid, but I took the bus and I was almost there when a man on the street, a total stranger, called me Topaz and started talking to me like he knew me and the name seemed too close to be a coincidence, and then I — I just couldn't talk to Mac after that."

"What upset you the night before?"

"A — a girl, a girl I didn't know, and she was bleeding, she was dead . . ." Risa bit her lip. "Please don't make me think about her."

"Finish your drink," Jim said. "I'll order another."

They had grilled tortuava caught that day and green chili burritos and flan for dessert.

Afterward Jim took her to Hussong's Cantina with its rough wood floor and old bar stools, seemingly unchanged from the early 1900's. Risa's head began to spin with the alcohol she had consumed, and when they left the cantina she bumped against Jim so that he had to hold her.

She giggled.

"You're drunk," he said.

She shook her head, then had to clutch at his arm. "Can't trust tequila," she said. "Sneaky."

They walked along the street to the car, Jim's arm around her.

"We'll have to stay here tonight," he said, "if you want to go back to that same beach to-morrow morning."

"All right," she said.

They came to the car and his arm tightened around her. She looked up at him though she could barely see his face in the dimly lit street.

"Risa," he said, then his mouth was on hers and she was swept by a golden fire that fused them together. When he held her at arm's length to stare into her eyes she felt incomplete.

"Jim," she murmured, snuggling against him again, raising her face.

After long moments he thrust her away again and shook her a little. "Damn it," he said, "you keep putting me into these situations. You must know how I feel about you, yet we've got this lost year between us. What if you're married? What if . . . ?"

The taste of ashes was in her mouth. How could she have forgotten Rory and what he meant to her? How could she let herself stay in Jim's arms and not think of the danger Rory might be in? She had even forgotten to look for his boat.

She disengaged herself from Jim. "I must find Rory," she said. "Nothing can be right until I do."

Jim said nothing. He helped her into the car in silence and they drove, without speaking, to a motel.

When Jim came out of the motel office, he handed her a key. "This is to your room," he said. "Please try to stay put." His voice was clipped, almost cold.

"Goodnight," she said.

When she lay in bed she tried not to think of the moments in Jim's arms and how she had responded. The day's confusion swirled chaotically in her head. And she was dizzy from the alcohol.

She propped herself on the pillows and stared at the wedge of light from the partly open bathroom door. She had been afraid to have the room completely dark but she couldn't sleep with too much light.

The trip with Rory to Baja is the wedge into the missing time, she told herself. I must try to think about it calmly, not panic because I imagined the dead girl.

Last November. I was feeling sad, still mourning Aunt Marie, missing her — she'd been dead only three weeks. It had been raining the day she died, a Monday. A fine drizzle, nasty and depressing. Aunt Marie and Rory had gone into town and when they came back I thought she looked tired, but I didn't think anything of it when she went into her room. She often rested in the afternoon. Rory disappeared into his room and I played the piano for hours, melancholy tunes in the minor keys — it was that kind of day.

Then when Beatrice went to tell Aunt Marie supper was ready, she rushed out of the room all upset and then we found out Marie was dead. "I told her a month ago," the doctor said. "She should have let you know."

But Rory had known, Aunt Marie had told him and they'd kept it from her so she would not worry, be upset. Her aunt had taken Rory to the bank that very afternoon and removed the contents from her safety deposit box to be available in case she did die as soon as the doctor thought she might. She had died even sooner than he expected. And so Rory had the will already. Aunt Marie was always well organized. He had gone through the other things she'd taken from the safety deposit box but said they were papers Aunt Marie might as well have thrown away, there was nothing of value . . .

Poor Aunt Marie. She had never had anything of value. Only the love of her sister's child and two months of marriage in her late years, beyond the time she might have had a child of her own. I did love her, Risa thought, but she was difficult to know. Her own grandmother had called Marie hardhearted and cold. But she wasn't. Just a private person, wanting no trespassing. How Rory's father had ever penetrated her privacy was beyond imagination. Certainly no other man ever

had. Though her aunt loved Rory, had left everything to him . . .

Rory. Why can't I think calmly of the Ferrari
and Rory behind the wheel? But when she
started to drift off into sleep and the Ferrari
loomed in her mind she cried out, forced herself
awake, heart pounding, afraid to go to sleep and
lose control of her thoughts.

✌ *12* ✌

Despite her efforts to stay awake, Risa dozed off. She spiraled down concentric circles of light into darkness, into a well of silence where no voice spoke, no sounds penetrated. Danger shared the darkness with her, a sense of being trapped made her beat blindly at unseen walls, then there were no walls and she fell into endless space, a yellow-brown sun shining far above her. If the sun's rays touched her something would happen, something she feared . . .

She jerked awake and stared around the shadowed room. A wedge of light came through a partly opened door and when she sat up in the bed she could see the door led to a bathroom. Where was she? Alarmed, she slid off the bed and groped for a light switch. There. But the room was unfamiliar even with the lights on. A bed, dresser, bedside table, brilliantly colored Mexican prints on the walls — she had never been in this room before. Shaken, she walked to the window and pulled aside the drape to look out into the night. Cars. Neon lights. A motel? Yes, she was in a motel.

What was she doing here? How had she gotten here? Bemused, she stared at the card of instructions for checking out and saw it was written in Spanish and English. Was she in Mexico?

And why was she sleeping in her bra and pants? Hurriedly she yanked on the clothes she found on a chair — a rust-colored pantsuit which fit perfectly. The brown shoes on the floor did too. They must be mine, she thought, but I've never seen them before. Her hand drifted to her head and she ran her fingers along the healed scar above her right ear.

She searched the room for a purse but found none. Then she felt in the pockets of the pants top. Money. Ten dollars and some change.

"I've got to get back to San Diego," she said aloud and was startled by the sound of her own voice. She opened the door and looked out. The motel was quiet, no sound came from any of the units, but the manager's office still showed a light inside. She closed the door softly behind her and walked as quietly as she could toward the office.

"Bus," she said to the sleepy-eyed man who answered her repeated ringing of the bell on the desk. "San Diego. Dónde es bus?"

He shook his head. "The bus to San Diego?" he repeated in heavily accented English. "The closest place is a café up the street. Open all night. The bus stops there, but it's the bus to Tijuana."

"That's fine," she said.

He stepped outside to point the direction.

She had seen a sign in his office: MOTEL CASA GRANDE, ENSENADA, B.C. She was in Mexico. As she hurried toward the Café Del Noche, she tried to remember how she'd gotten here. But the last clear memory she had was getting in the van with Rhoddie and Gill. Blue, their big black dog, had to stay behind and howled mournfully from the end of his chain. Where were they going? There had been no gray van in the motel parking area. Anyway she couldn't imagine Rhoddie and Gill staying in a motel. They would sleep in the van.

"Café," she said to the man behind the counter as she slid onto a stool. "Café con leche."

She waited until he brought the coffee and then she asked, "Tijuana bus — cuándo?"

He shrugged. "Temprano o tarde," he said and grinned, then repeated the words in English. "Bus come sooner or later."

She sighed and took a sip of bitter coffee. Okay, she thought, try again to remember. The three of us were in the van. Gill driving, Rhoddie in the middle, I got in last and closed the door. Rhoddie asked me if I had to work this Saturday. She could hear Rhoddie's warm, deep voice in her ears, ". . . 'cause Gill and I are going to the desert, Kitty, and you won't have a ride home."

"I'll find one," she had said, then Gill had chimed in, laughing at her.

"Hey, listen to little old Kitty." And she had flushed, ashamed that Gill realized she would rather walk miles than accept a ride from someone she didn't know well.

Kitty looked at the man behind the café counter. "What day is it?" she asked.

"Tuesday. No, is Wednesday now." His dark eyes regarded her with interest. "You run away from your man?"

"What? Oh, no, no." She shook her head and stared down into her coffee cup to discourage conversation. Surely she had not come to Ensenada with a man, she wouldn't do anything like that. Besides, she had been alone in the motel room. But it had been Thursday in San Diego when the three of them started out for somewhere in the gray van. Thursday. And now she was in Mexico and it was Wednesday. What had happened to the week between?

She had met Gill and Rhoddie in Mexico. Over a year ago now. But she shied away from thinking about that meeting, she never thought about it if she could help herself. And she hadn't been down to Baja since then. Why was she here now?

The urge to run from the café, flee somewhere else, anywhere else, almost overcame her. She clutched the sides of the stool and closed her eyes, fighting the impulse. Wait for the bus, she told herself, repeating the sentence over and over to cover up the word "run" that seemed to flash off and on in her mind like a neon sign.

"You okay?" The man was leaning across the counter, his hand touched her shoulder. She jerked back, almost falling off the stool.

"The bus." He pointed toward the café door.

Kitty took a deep breath. "Gracias," she said. She knew he watched her as she walked out.

As the bus rattled along, she put her head back and tried to relax but could not. What had happened between Thursday and Wednesday? Why didn't she remember? Was this amnesia? But she knew her name, knew she was Kitty Morgan and she knew where she lived too, with Rhoddie and Gill in San Diego. She had stared at her own face in the dingy café mirror and saw the familiar short curly hair, the brown eyes. Her hand went up — yes, the scar was there, too. But the clothes weren't hers. She slid her fingers over the pants. Good quality, expensive. Somewhat soiled here and there but obviously new just the same.

Amnesia. No, she wouldn't think about it, she had built her life slowly, pulled herself together during the past year. She had a job, she was getting over her fears, Rhoddie was a good friend and Gill had been leaving her alone lately, so even that was not a problem.

Her life had been going along smoothly. Not exciting, but she didn't need excitement, she was safe with Rhoddie looking out for her, there had been no nightmares during the last few months.

The day lightened slowly. Clouds obscured the sky so she did not see the sunrise, and she shivered in the chill dawn breeze at Tijuana. Her shirt was long-sleeved but she had no coat. Funny she would not have brought a coat. After all, it was November and the nights were cold. She walked across the border to the U.S. and got on a San Diego bus.

Not much money left, but enough to catch a city transit bus after she got downtown. She dozed a little on the drive up, waking every few minutes with a start and looking around her to make sure she was still on the bus. Several hours passed before she was out of the last bus and climbing the hill to where she lived. Blue's deep, threatening bark reached her before she saw him.

"Blue," she said, "don't carry on so. It's only me."

His bark changed, became higher pitched, and he flung himself at her in greeting. He was off the chain so Rhoddie must be home although the gray van wasn't parked in the drive.

Kitty stood looking at the old shingled house for a moment. It needed paint and the avocado trees crowded around it and hung over the roof as if to hide its shabbiness. The house was early California bungalow style, a good-sized place, and despite all the inconveniences Kitty loved it.

She fondled the dog's floppy black ears. "Good old Blue," she said. "Did you miss me?"

The door flew open and Rhoddie rushed out. She had on her painting jeans and sweat shirt, streaked with many paint colors and smelling of turpentine. Her long dark hair was caught back with an elastic.

"Kitty," she cried. "Where on earth have you been the past week?"

Kitty shook her head. "I just got back from

Ensenada but I don't know how I got there."

"Oh, no," Rhoddie said. "You don't think you . . ."

"I don't know what happened," Kitty said hurriedly. "The last I remember, the three of us were getting into the van and Blue was howling because he couldn't go along."

"But that was last Thursday," Kitty said, her voice higher pitched than usual. "You mean you drew a blank again? After all this time?"

Kitty twisted her hands together. "I must have."

"You mean you don't remember the accident at all, that car forcing us off the road, that damn nut in the sports car, and then going to the hospital? You mean you don't remember this?" Rhoddie thrust out her left arm, pulling up the shirt sleeve, and for the first time Kitty saw she wore a cast on the arm from hand to elbow.

"You broke your arm?"

"Yes, I broke my arm and you were out cold, you must have hit your head, and the ambulance took us to Sharp Hospital Emergency Room because it was the closest. And they wheeled you in there and I thought you were dead. Later, when they told me you were gone, that you'd disappeared, I was sure at first that you *had* died and they just didn't want to tell me. They finally had to give me a shot to get this cast on and Gill . . ." She paused.

"Did he get hurt?"

"No. Not a scratch. Even the van wasn't too

bad. Squashed up some but Gill was able to drive it to a body shop."

"I — I don't recall any of it, Rhoddie. I did notice some scabs on my hands but they're healed now. My head's all right."

Rhoddie came closer. "Where'd you get the clothes?" she asked. Her yellow eyes stared into Kitty's. "You didn't have any money when we left on Thursday because you left your purse home. Where's your car coat and your other clothes?"

"Oh, Rhoddie, I haven't any idea." Kitty fingered the rust pantsuit. "I've never seen these things before either. What shall I do?"

"First of all, why don't you come in and change into other clothes. Maybe you'll feel better. Was there — were you with anyone in Baja?"

Kitty shook her head.

"Joe King called me," Rhoddie said over her shoulder as they went into the house. "He wanted to know why you didn't show."

"Oh, my God," Kitty said. "I didn't show up for work? I'll bet he was mad."

Rhoddie looked at her curiously. "You mean you don't remember if you went to work or not? You didn't, Joe says so. But you didn't know?"

"I haven't got a single memory of the time between getting into the van last Thursday and now. What did Joe say?"

"I told him you'd been in an accident and I forgot to call him and you'd be out maybe a week, we'd let him know. He was upset but he'll get over it."

"Thanks, Rhoddie."

"Gill's been out looking for you. I think he's pretty shook by the whole thing — he's been acting strange."

"I've caused a lot of trouble," Kitty said.

Rhoddie shrugged. "Not your fault. Are you hungry? Want some coffee?"

"As soon as I change." Kitty went into her bedroom and selected a complete change of clothes, took them into the bathroom and showered before she dressed. When she came into the kitchen, Rhoddie had made a fresh pot of coffee.

"You've been painting," Kitty commented as she pushed the toaster lever down. "What are you doing now?"

"Oh, landscapes again. As a matter of fact, I was trying to get that stretch of beach below Salsipuedes, you know . . ." Her voice trailed off.

Kitty picked the toast out and began to butter the slices. "Where you found me," she said, her voice calm, not betraying the inner shudder, the fright she always felt when they talked about the Baja beach where she had met Rhoddie and Gill. Suddenly her eyes widened and she jumped up from her chair and rushed into the bedroom. Was it gone? Had she taken the topaz brooch with her last Thursday and lost it somewhere?

But the topaz glowed at her from the yellow jewel box Rhoddie had given her for a Christmas present. Kitty picked up the brooch and held it in her hands, the gem seeming to warm her, as always.

"What . . . ?" Rhoddie appeared in the doorway. "Oh, the brooch. Did you think you'd lost it?"

"I — I didn't know," Kitty said. "You mentioned painting the beach and I guess I . . ."

"I won't ever forget that night," Rhoddie said. Kitty flinched inwardly, half afraid to listen to a retelling and yet fascinated, as though she had been a bystander rather than a participant.

"You know, if it hadn't been for Blue we never would have found you in that crevice." Rhoddie always told the story the same way. "He just kept barking and Gill kept yelling at him until finally I couldn't stand either of them and got out of the sleeping bag to see what was bugging Blue."

"That's the first I remember," Kitty said, her own compulsion to relive the incident forcing her to respond. "This big black dog licking my face."

"Blue's always liked you, ever since the first. You were an awful mess, your hair all caked with blood, your face streaked with it, your clothes all torn, crying and moaning and clutching that topaz brooch in your hand like it was all you had in the world."

"But you took care of me," Kitty said.

"Yeah, but it was Gill that was smart enough to pack up and drive the van out of there when I brought you back."

"He didn't want to take me."

"Well, he's like that. You know, Gill's okay but he likes the easy way of doing things. Anyway, we did bring you along. I sure hated to chop off all your long hair but the cut was nasty, took a while to heal."

Kitty's hand went to her head, felt the scar. "I'm still not sure why you took so much trouble. You fed me, bought me clothes, put up with me when I was scared to go out of the house . . ."

Rhoddie shrugged. "You're paying your way now. And I wouldn't leave anyone to get shut up in one of those Mexicano jails. You might have died there."

"You think yet I was with that freaked-out group you told me about, the ones who had been on the beach earlier that night?"

"What else? You must have been stoned on something, they all were, and then there was that awful racket and they all cleared out. I don't know if you fell or there really was an accident like Gill claims there was. But they just went and left you. The shape they were in, they probably haven't missed you yet."

"But you'd think I could have remembered something in all this time."

"You knew your name. That's the first thing Gill asked you, 'What's your name?' and you stared down at the topaz and you said, 'Kitty, Kitty, Kitty,' three times in a row and he said, 'Kitty what?' and you said, 'Kitty Morgan,' and passed out cold, right at his feet."

Kitty shivered. "Why do you think I went back, Rhoddie? Went back down to Ensenada and don't remember getting there?"

"Beats me. Maybe you started to recall something from before. I always figured you'd been on one of those drugs that affects the brain and I figure maybe someday you'll remember. But if you don't, so what? You're doing okay — they love you down at The Copper King. You've got friends, a place to live. You're a good-looking girl . . ."

"Well, well." Gill's voice. Kitty turned to see him standing in the doorway. "So Miss High and Mighty is back. I suppose you'll say you never saw me before, that I'm a perfect stranger like you did the other day in Del Mar."

❧ *13* ❧

Kitty stared at Gill uncomprehendingly. She didn't like looking at him, didn't really like Gill despite the fact he had helped her. A beard covered the lower half of his face, straggling down onto his chest, his eyes so pale a blue as to seem misplaced in the tanned face.

"I — don't understand you," she said.

"In Del Mar, down on the beach below that house you were staying in. Wow, some place that was. Money for sure."

"I haven't been to Del Mar, I don't know anyone there." Kitty spoke uncertainly, aware she could have been anywhere in the missing week.

"Oh, Gill, leave her alone. She's had a blackout. Doesn't remember the accident we had or the hospital. First thing she knew it was today and she was in Mexico." Rhoddie paused, moved closer to Gill and grabbed his arm. "Hey — how come you didn't tell me about Del Mar? Was Kitty really there or are you picking on her again?"

"Yeah, well, I didn't want to say anything to you in case she was pulling some weirdo deal. She acted peculiar. Didn't know me, or said she didn't."

"How did you find her in Del Mar?"

134

"Followed her," Gill said to Rhoddie. "When I got the van going again I drove to Sharp because the ambulance dudes said they were going there, and I get to the parking lot and here's this guy carrying Kitty, she's still out cold. So I watch and the first thing I know she's getting in a car with him and they take off. So I followed them, saw her go into this place in Del Mar. I came back to Sharp to find out about you and, man, you were all shook, they were holding you down and you were screaming . . ."

"I knew something was wrong," Rhoddie said. "Kitty wouldn't simply disappear."

Kitty looked from one to the other of them. "I can't — I can't recall any of that, Gill. Not the man or the house in Del Mar or meeting you on the beach."

A tiny smile quirked the corners of Gill's mouth. "It's okay, now I know what gives. I thought you were trying to con me."

Kitty glanced down at the brooch in her hand, then took it in her fingers and pinned it to the left side of her shirt, over her heart.

"Joe King likes your gimmick," Gill said. "He thinks you're a comer. I stopped by last weekend and the regulars were all bent out of shape because he had a substitute."

Kitty shook her head. "All Rhoddie's idea," she said. "I wouldn't have applied for the piano-bar job in the first place, much less called myself Topaz."

Rhoddie grinned. "And you sure fought those

low-necked dresses I picked out for you."

Kitty smiled weakly. She still hadn't gotten used to the gowns Rhoddie insisted she wear, exposing half her breasts, it seemed to her. But when she pinned the topaz brooch at the vee of one of the long gowns, either the brown or the pale yellow — she wore no other colors — she also knew the result was good showmanship. The mirror told her she was alluring, the audience response told Joe King she was worth keeping on at the piano bar. Kitty hoped her playing was good too, but she realized the way she looked, the image she projected, was certainly part of her success.

"Topaz, the Untouchable," Gill said. "So what were you doing in Mexico?"

"I was near the beach at Salsipuedes. I don't know why."

"You go with that guy?"

"What guy?"

"The one in the orange Porsche."

Kitty twisted her hands together. "I don't know who it is, I don't even know who you're talking about."

"Gill, quit picking on her. I figure her problem's like before. She's never gotten back any memory of her life before that night on the beach in Baja. She fell that night and hit her head. She got it hit again in the accident last Thursday. So she wandered around in a daze for a while. Maybe she'll remember, maybe she won't. What's the difference? She's okay, she's back home. So some guy took her to his house. Big deal."

"Wasn't his house," Gill said. "This guy went back to San Diego. I followed him to an office in Clairmont. He's a doctor. Dr. James Halloway. And he doesn't live in Del Mar."

"You did all that running around while I was still in the emergency room?" Rhoddie demanded.

Gill shrugged. "You were okay. I figured you'd like to know about Kitty."

"But you didn't tell me any of this until now."

Gill shrugged again. "Well, I would have. Just happens I lost track of her so I didn't see the point in mentioning anything."

"Who does live in the house in Del Mar, Gill?" Kitty asked.

"Some dude named Rory Robertson."

"Did you talk to him?" Rhoddie demanded.

"He wasn't home."

"Does the name mean anything to you, Kitty?"

Kitty shook her head. Her mind was confused. Strange places, names she didn't know, how could she have been where Gill said she was and not remember? Her head had begun to ache. "I have to rest for a while," she said. "Do you think Joe King will want me to work tonight?"

"I'll call him," Rhoddie said. "You take it easy."

"Wait a minute," Gill said. "There's some more . . ."

"Not now. Let her go to sleep. You can see she's dead on her feet." Rhoddie yanked at Gill's arm. "We can talk later."

Kitty stretched out on her bed and pulled up the brown-and-yellow afghan Rhoddie had made for her. Rhoddie took care of her almost as though she was a child and Rhoddie was her mother. But she's only a few years older than I am, Kitty thought. I'm too dependent, that's the trouble. Gill certainly is no father figure, though. Thank God he's quit trying to make love to me. There was a bad period a few months back when I thought I would have to leave this house and find another place to live.

"I'm getting out," she had told Gill. "You know I don't want any part of you and yet you won't stop pestering me. So I'm leaving. You can explain it to Rhoddie."

"Oh, come on, Kitty," Gill said. "It was just for laughs — you know. No need to get uptight, no need at all to cut out on us. Forget it."

And he had not bothered her again, not that way. She had never told Rhoddie and certainly Gill wouldn't. But now he picked at Kitty, little mean remarks, every put-down he could find. She wondered sometimes if he really hated her for refusing him and also for occupying so much room in Rhoddie's life, where before there had been only Gill.

I can't trust him, she decided. He would like to see me gone, yet he hasn't found a way to accomplish it without making Rhoddie mad. Did he follow me to Del Mar or is he making up a story?

Kitty turned over and tucked the afghan more closely about herself. Rhoddie is my friend, she thought, but she can't help me remember, no one can. I didn't think it would happen again. The wall has always been there, no memories before the night on the beach in Baja. But I got used to having the block, it didn't matter so much because I had a home here and I like my job, the customers like me too, and I'm somebody — I'm Topaz, besides being Kitty Morgan.

Gill's words came back to her. Topaz, the Untouchable. And not just with Gill. She could joke with the men at the piano bar, laugh and talk to them as long as she was playing the piano, was Topaz, the entertainer. But when she got up off the piano bench and was Kitty Morgan she was finished with them, thank you. No drinks, no dates, no taking her home. No, thanks.

Joe King said it was good for business, he didn't mind. Rhoddie said Kitty would get over it, don't worry, don't force anything. Wait. Some man would come along sometime and Kitty would feel differently. After all, look how far she had come in a year.

Now she would take the bus to work when Rhoddie or Gill couldn't bring her, whereas in the beginning she was frozen with fear every time she left their house. She still hated to find a ride home at night, after work, when the buses were not running. Most often she took a taxi if

Rhoddie or Gill couldn't pick her up.

"That's so damn expensive," Gill said. "You got fifty guys every night with their tongues hanging out to take you home."

"It's my money," Kitty said, always with a sense of wonder and pride that she was able to earn as much as she did — quite a bit, with tips — merely for playing the piano and sometimes singing in her husky, untrained voice.

"I'm not a singer," she told Rhoddie.

"Yeah, but you come across sexy," Rhoddie insisted. "That counts too."

Rhoddie *was* a singer. With Gill playing guitar, they made the restaurant circuit each season and were as popular in their way as Kitty in hers. Rhoddie also sold some of her paintings each year and taught art classes, but Gill didn't work except when he played guitar with Rhoddie.

The three of them lived in the hills to the east of San Diego, in the old house in the equally old avocado grove where Blue could have space to run. Kitty loved the house. She had her own large bedroom and private use of the bathroom near it because Rhoddie and Gill slept in the other end of the house. They were buying the property and Kitty knew her rent payments helped. She had felt a part of a family until Gill began his advances. Now that he disliked her the harmony was broken.

Kitty shifted restlessly. There was another wall to contend with, a shut-off space really, encompassing a lost week. Gill had insisted a man drove her to Del Mar. A pulse throbbed in her neck. A doctor, Gill said. She couldn't imagine herself getting into a car and driving off with a strange man. Gill must be lying.

Her hand came up to touch the topaz on her breast. Odd that the stone would seem warm when she felt it, as though the sun's rays had entered deep into the heart of the topaz and were trapped there forever. The feel of the gem under her fingers made her relax. Everything's all right, she thought sleepily. I'm safe . . .

She was in a hidden spot, safe at last from her pursuer. She lay quietly, not worrying because no one could find her here among the secret rocks where the gold-brown sun bathed her in amber light. She was inside the topaz, concealed from the world. Safe . . .

A sense of something next to her, her face touched roughly, wetness . . . Kitty jerked awake.

"I sent Blue in to wake you up." Rhoddie's voice and Blue's paws on the bed, his wet tongue licking her face.

Kitty pushed him away and sat up. "Hey, you monster, get lost," she said to the dog.

"You've got a few minutes to eat before you go to work," Rhoddie said.

"What time is it?" For the first time Kitty noticed the overhead light in her bedroom was on. "Did I sleep all day?"

"You sure did. And Joe says come play ye olde

piano and welcome back. Everyone has missed you."

Kitty ate clam chowder with a corned beef sandwich, drank two cups of coffee, then dressed herself in the long gown of brown chiffon, pinned the topaz brooch in the vee between her breasts. She ran a brush through her short curls and touched her lips with apricot lip gloss, checked the result in the mirror. Some eye shadow? A pale green tonight, yes. "Okay," she said to Rhoddie, "here's Topaz." She caught up a brown shawl and they went out to the van, where Gill was waiting.

He dropped Rhoddie off first at the Woman's Center, where she taught a class in painting. As soon as he had maneuvered the van back into traffic, he said to Kitty, "So you aren't going to tell her about the money."

"What money?"

"Are you kidding? You mean you honestly don't know any of this, you actually flipped out for a week?"

"Gill, I'm not playing any games. I don't know about Del Mar or money or anything at all except I woke up in Ensenada early this morning. And I'd rather not talk about it if you don't mind."

"Yeah, well, Kitty . . ." his voice trailed off. She glanced at him, saw he was chewing his lip. He hunched his shoulders, shifted uneasily.

"What's the matter?"

"You ever felt anyone is after you?"

"After me? What are you talking about?"

"You know, like out to get you, hurt you. Like that. I remember how scared you used to be to go anywhere, we practically had to pry you out of the house."

"I'm getting over that."

"Yeah. But is someone after you?"

Kitty thought of her dreams, her nightmares where a stranger pursued her, an unknown whose touch would be death. "I — I don't think so, no," she said quickly. "Why?"

"Oh, no special reason." Gill's voice was higher pitched than usual, his laugh forced. "I guess I'm just worried about you blacking out." He pulled into the parking lot of The Copper King. "Don't ride home with anyone you don't know tonight," he said. "I'll be here to pick you up."

She flashed an incredulous glance at Gill as she got out of the van. Don't ride with a stranger? Why on earth would she?

"Thanks," she said.

Joe King was there himself, a rarity this early in the evening. He took her hand. Let it go. "You're a bit pale, still. Are you all right?"

She smiled at him. He was fiftyish and she suspected his hair didn't remain that black without aid, but his dark eyes snapped with vigor. "I feel fine. I'm sorry I had to let you down."

"None of us can control accidents. I'm happy you weren't injured any worse than you were. And not just for business reasons." He patted her shoulder but took his hand away immediately. Joe had made a mild pass at her soon after she started work there, and when she had made it clear she couldn't stay on if he persisted, he had not tried again, seemed now to respect her idiosyncrasies about being touched. "You're a nice girl," he added. "I wouldn't like to see you hurt."

Kitty put away her shawl, settled into being Topaz. She sat on the piano bench and immediately patrons began to drift to the piano bar by twos and threes. "Didn't expect you tonight. What a neat surprise," the voices said. "Where've you been?" "Hey, I missed you."

She began to play, the old tunes first, "Stardust," "Lover Come Back to Me," then slipped into more current songs. "Make believe you love me," she sang softly, "for the good times . . ."

She felt at home here, comfortable, in the swirl of smoke, the clinking of glasses. She did not smoke herself or drink while she performed, except lemonade. The standard joke — "A very dry lemonade for Topaz." The group around the piano bar liked her, she liked them, they all enjoyed themselves.

But tonight something went wrong. She had slipped into the Topaz role, started to relax, everything was smooth. Then after her first break, after she reseated herself, started to play a song about a green-eyed lady, she felt uneasy. Eyes, somewhere in the room watching her, cold and inimical. Hostile eyes. She shivered and touched the topaz between songs, but its warmth did not ease the chill inside.

What had Gill asked her? "Is someone out to get you?"

She shook her head impatiently. She must be imagining things. But the feel of unseen eyes stayed with her.

❧ *14* ❧

Kitty thought the evening would never end. She tried to hide herself behind a screen of music, tried to dampen her awareness with sound, but the unseen watcher remained at the edge of her mind, waiting.

Who is it? Kitty asked herself. Someone I know? She tried to deny the other thoughts crowding into her mind. Someone from the past from behind the wall, the unremembered time. Would she know him? Who were these men Gill mentioned — the doctor who had taken her to Del Mar in his car and the man who owned the house where she had stayed? Two different names, names she had not recognized.

The person who was here tonight wished her no good fortune. Kitty could sense the malevolence flowing toward her, the topaz glowed warm between her breasts as if to ward off the ill-wishing.

Rhoddie had never seen a topaz as large as the one in the brooch. The entire ornament was as big as a silver dollar, though not round, more oval in shape. And the gem itself was quarter-sized, or would be if it were round.

To Kitty the topaz was her talisman, her hold on a tenuous reality. But Rhoddie became fascinated with the stone. "It must be worth a chunk of money," she told Kitty, but Kitty didn't care about the money.

Rhoddie had dug up all she could from the library. "No wonder you're so hung up on that topaz," she said. "According to legend the topaz protects the wearer from harm — but only if you were born at the right time. What's your birth date?"

"November," Kitty said without thinking. "November twentieth."

They stared at each other. "You remembered something," Rhoddie said.

Kitty's heart leapt in fear and anticipation but nothing else came back to her, not even how old she was.

"Well," Rhoddie went on, "that's the right month, the topaz is your birthstone. Another thing it's supposed to do is prevent evil dreams, keep them from happening. Maybe you ought to wear it to bed to get rid of those nightmares."

She was half kidding, but Kitty did put the brooch under her pillow and though the bad dreams still came she would partly rouse and touch the topaz and when she drifted back to sleep she slept peacefully.

Bits and pieces of what Rhoddie told her came back now through the music as she played. "Light my fire," she sang, "come on, baby . . ." Fire. Topaz meant fire, but the fire of the sun, the golden warmth.

Her hands began a new song. "I need a friend," she sang. "Oh, Lord . . ." What was the little poem? Something about a friend. The topaz brought friends, the topaz had brought her Rhoddie . . .

> *Who first comes to this world below*
> *With drear November's fog and snow*
> *Should prize the topaz's amber hue,*
> *Emblem of friends and lovers true.*

Yes, the topaz had brought her a friend. But not a lover. Unless one of the men Gill talked of . . . No, she would remember love, you couldn't forget love. Tears pricked her eyes. Words came into her head. "A topaz for my Lady Fair . . ." Her fingers faltered on the keys and she missed a note. Those words meant something. What did they mean? Not from Rhoddie's research — she knew all that by heart. This was different. Where had the line come from? A spasm of pain made her drop her head, then hands were on her shoulders, Joe King's voice in her ears.

"Enough for tonight. Don't overdo. Go home to bed, let me know how you feel tomorrow."

She tried to smile at Joe but sobs choked her and she had all she could do to fight them back.

Voices rose in protest as she left the piano but Joe stayed there and talked to them while Kitty made her way through the room to the big bar. Gill usually waited here but she didn't see him. She slid onto the last stool, the one past the bargirl's station. The bartender moved down to say hello.

"Hi, Rocky. Could you call a taxi for me? And maybe mix me a screwdriver?"

"Sure. Can do. You leaving early?"

Kitty nodded, took a deep breath. She no longer felt the menace of unseen eyes, she had probably only imagined them, a leftover from last spring when she was afraid of everything. And the words in her head tonight — useless to cry over words from behind the wall, their meaning unknown. But I mind not knowing, she thought. There's a feeling to go with those words and it touched me tonight but I couldn't grasp it and now the feeling is gone and I — I can hardly bear the loss. She blinked to keep back the tears.

"Yellow Cab's coming," Rocky said. "Here's your screwdriver."

"Thanks."

"You know, a funny thing, a little while ago there was a guy sitting right there where you are. He was asking about you, said he didn't think you worked here anymore. I said sure you did and he asked if you'd been sick and I gave him the who-knows bit. Good-looking guy, dressed like money. Thought maybe he wanted to meet you, but he didn't ask. Then Gill came in and I started to talk to him and when I looked back the guy had left. Gill took off right after him. I got the notion maybe Gill was following him, 'cause he left his beer. Gill never does that. You know anything about it?"

Kitty shook her head, pulled the shawl closer. Someone *had* been watching her then. A stranger. And Gill had followed him? She shivered. Her nightmares where an unseen pursuer menaced her for unknown reasons were coming true.

When the cab let her off in front of the house she heard Blue's welcoming bark with disappointment — he was still on the chain, no one was home. Kitty unhooked him and brought him into the house. Rhoddie was usually home by now. But if Gill had not been there to pick Rhoddie up . . .

She fixed herself a bowl of soup, fed the dog an old hotdog she found in the refrigerator, and then tried to read but wasn't able to concentrate. She moved restlessly from one chair to another, unsettling Blue, who was trying to nap. He eyed her movements for a while, then turned his back to her and curled up. Finally she took Gill's guitar and began to try random chords. She didn't play well yet but enjoyed learning.

She knew music, knew it so well Rhoddie was sure Kitty had been to a music school sometime. Somewhere. She played the piano without needing music, knowing seemingly innumerable songs by memory. Others she worked out in short order as soon as she had the melody. And one night at The Copper King somebody had brought in a flute and she found she could handle a flute very well. Yes, she knew music — from her past behind the wall.

Gill's guitar playing was superb, he was teaching her flamenco a few months ago before their relationship had deteriorated. Kitty began trying the flamenco beat, gradually becoming absorbed in what she was doing. She didn't even notice when Blue's head came up, but she heard the low warning growl and her fingers left the guitar strings as she watched the dog.

He got to his feet and strode stiff-legged to the door, his hackles up. He had been trained not to bark inside the house but his deep, reverberating growl filled the room. Someone was at the door. Why didn't they ring the bell?

Was that a knock she heard? Yes, someone was tapping gently against the heavy oak front door. Kitty moved to stand beside the dog. She peered through a high side window, climbing on a chest to see. There was a man on the stoop outside the door. She could not see his face well but he didn't look familiar.

I won't open the door, she thought. Her hand was on Blue's collar and though he had stopped growling, the hair along his back was still up. Then she shook her head. What was there to be afraid of with this great black beast standing next to her? Blue would intimidate anyone. But she hesitated. The man had been wearing a stocking cap. It wasn't very cold out — not that cold. And hadn't he carried something in his hand?

I'd better climb up and look again, she told herself, but even as she dithered, Blue's tail began to wag and he whined happily. When she was on the chest once more and could see out the side window, there was no one on the doorstep but the gray van was pulling into the driveway. Gill and Rhoddie were home.

"Did you see anyone? A man in a stocking cap?" she asked as they came through the door.

Gill's head swiveled around and he went outside again.

"I didn't see a soul," Rhoddie said. "You haven't been imagining things like you used to, have you?"

Kitty shook her head impatiently. "Blue heard him and growled when he knocked at the door."

"Did you open it?"

"No. I don't know — he didn't look right somehow, and then you came home and he disappeared."

Gill came back inside and closed the door. "No one out there now. What did he look like?"

"I couldn't tell much out of that little window, only that he was a stranger and he wore a stocking cap."

"Sounds weird," Rhoddie said.

Gill said nothing and Kitty thought he acted upset. She remembered what Rocky had said.

"Is he the man you were following?" she asked Gill.

"What? What are you talking about?"

"Rocky told me there was a man in the bar tonight asking about me. Then you came in and the man left and you went after him."

Rhoddie narrowed her eyes and stared at Gill. "I knew you were holding out on me. Give."

"I need a beer," Gill said. "Can't we all sit down?"

Rhoddie jerked her head toward the kitchen. "In there," she said.

Gill sat at the kitchen table and fondled the can of beer. "You know about the accident," he said.

"Naturally. Get on with it." Rhoddie's voice was harsh.

"No, I meant her." Gill pointed at Kitty. "You said she didn't remember."

Kitty glanced at the cast on Rhoddie's arm. "Rhoddie told me. She said a sports car forced the van off the road and it overturned and she broke her arm and I was knocked unconscious but you weren't hurt."

"Yeah. Well . . ." Gill shifted in his seat. "I got a look at the driver of that gold sports car and he had red hair."

Both the women stared at him blankly.

"So?" Rhoddie said.

"It doesn't mean anything to me," Kitty added.

Gill was somewhat deflated. He glanced at Kitty. "I thought you might remember something."

She shook her head.

"Just so happens I talked to a red-headed guy in The Copper King a couple of days before we got forced off the road," Gill went on. "And he was in there tonight. That's Rocky's guy. The very same one. Sure I followed him but he

153

slipped away from me, the old van can't match those foreign jobs."

"What did he want?" Rhoddie asked. "You talked to him. What did he want that night?"

"Yeah. Well . . ." Gill scratched his beard, took a drink of beer. "Like tonight. He asked about Kitty? Only he didn't call her Kitty, he called her Topaz like he didn't know her name, really. So I figured he was some guy wanted to meet her, they all do. But he says he's seen her talk to me, seen her get in my van and wants to know if we're married. I laughed like hell and told him no way — the field was clear if he was interested."

"So was he?" Rhoddie asked.

"Not exactly. He — uh — he said I didn't sound as though I liked Topaz too well and I . . ."

"Get on with it. We all three know what was bugging you about Kitty?"

Both Gill and Kitty looked at Rhoddie in surprise. She had never given any indication she had noticed Gill's advances or Kitty's rejection of them.

Rhoddie shrugged. "I knew you'd get over it in time if I left the subject alone. So now it's out in the air. So what else is new?"

Gill's face had reddened. Kitty stared down at the floor.

"Okay," Gill said, "I told the guy she was a cold little bitch and the sooner she got out of my house and my life the better I'd like it."

Kitty winced at his words.

154

"Anyway, he gave me some money."

"For what?"

"To — to help get rid of Kitty."

Rhoddie got to her feet. "Gillman Townsend! Do you mean you took money to — to kill Kitty?"

Gill moved his shoulders uneasily, ran his fingers through his hair. "Oh, hell, Rhoddie, you know I wouldn't have hurt her. Not really. I thought maybe I could scare her into going, then she'd be gone, the guy wouldn't know where, so it would all work out. I wasn't going to hurt her, damn it."

"No, just frighten her to death. Gill, how could you?" Tears rolled down Rhoddie's face. "Oh, Gill how could you?" She slumped back into her chair and Gill reached to touch her shoulder, but she jerked away.

"Anyway, I didn't do a damn thing to her, not a thing." Gill's voice was sullen. "Then that red-haired bastard must have decided to do us all in. He's the guy that forced us off the road. It was sheer luck we didn't go all the way down the embankment onto the freeway below." He shook his head. "He meant to kill all of us. Kitty for some reason I don't even know. Me because I took his lousy money and he figured I could recognize him, could tell someone about him. But you . . ." Gill spread his hands open in front of Rhoddie. "There was no damn reason in the world for him to want you dead — you just happened to be along. He's not human, thinking like that."

Kitty sat frozen in position. It was all true, all her terrible dreams, all her fears of leaving the house. A stranger wanted her dead, had tried to kill her and she didn't know why. If he succeeded she wouldn't even know why she had to die.

"Aw, Rhoddie," Gill was saying, "I don't ever want anyone but you. When that bastard tried to kill you too, I made up my mind to get him, clobber him good, and throw the whole damn five hundred dollars in his face after I smashed it in first. But I didn't have the money. She had it."

"What?" Kitty's head came up, she looked into Gill's pale blue eyes.

"You had the envelope with the money. After the accident, I shoved the envelope in your coat pocket, your car coat that was lying on the seat. You were stretched out on the ground, Rhoddie was in too much pain to notice. I knew the cops would be there and I've been hassled by cops before, I didn't want the money on me, maybe they'd think it was stolen, I don't know, I just got panicky. How in hell was I to know Rhoddie was going to throw the damn coat over you the last thing, and then off the money went with you to the hospital."

"I don't have any five hundred dollars," Kitty said slowly.

"You did for a while there. When you took off from the hospital I had to follow you to get the money back." His voice was bitter. "Otherwise you could have gone, and welcome."

"I don't understand," Kitty said. Had she really had the money? Is that what she had used to buy new clothes and go to Mexico during the lost week? Had she spent it all?

"You gave the money back to me at Del Mar," Gill said. "You were down on the beach and I followed you and asked you for it and you pulled the envelope out of your coat pocket and handed it to me."

"I can't remember . . ."

Gill shrugged. "Maybe so. I can't figure you out." He looked back at Rhoddie. "So I got the money and then Kitty shows up here again and when I go to The Copper King tonight there's that red-headed s-o-b at the bar. He saw me and took off so I didn't get him. But I will."

"If he doesn't get us first," Rhoddie said. "He must have been the man at the door, wearing a cap to cover the red hair. You know any red-heads, Kitty?"

"No. But he's really only after me. I'll leave." She swallowed, forced the words out. "I'll go away from here where he can't find me, and as soon as he realizes I'm gone he'll leave you two alone."

"Don't talk like that," Rhoddie said, but her voice was strained. Gill's blue eyes were as cold as ice.

They want me to go, Kitty said to herself. And I must. But I'm so afraid. Where will I go? What will I do?

Alone in her bedroom Kitty was restless, unable to relax. Ideas, fragments of plans darted in and out of her mind. Buy a suitcase. Take the money she had saved out of the bank. But there was nothing she could do until morning. Blue was outside to warn of any strangers near the house. Rhoddie and Gill were inside. Stop opening drawers and pulling clothes off hangers. Go to bed. Rest.

She put on her nightgown, slid under the covers, pulled the yellow-and-brown afghan up. The feel of the wool under her fingers made her eyes fill with tears. She would have to leave Rhoddie, the only friend she had. What have I done in the past that someone would want to kill me? she wondered.

"Why don't you go see a shrink?" Gill had suggested more than once. "You can go to Mental Health at University Hospital, doesn't cost you."

"I'm afraid," she had always said. "I can't go."

I should have done what Gill suggested, she thought now. I can't keep the wall between myself and the past forever. It's dangerous.

She began to play the familiar game with no answers. How old am I, really? Twenty-one like we decided, Rhoddie and I, because I needed to be that old to get the job at The Copper King?

Do I have any parents, any brothers or sisters? Was I married? Did I have a lover? Is that why I can't form any relationship with a man now? Did I really take drugs, travel with a freaked-out group? Is that why I was on the Baja beach?

Now it was too late to seek help from a psychiatrist, at least one in San Diego. An unknown figure from the past had reached out for her and she must flee, hide. She must go or die.

Her hand sought the security of the topaz brooch she had put under her pillow. The topaz was from the past, something good from the past. Whoever gave this to me loved me, she told herself, as she had many times before. The topaz warms and comforts me, it came from one who loved me. What were the words she had remembered tonight? "A topaz for my Lady Fair . . ." She fell asleep with the words in her mind.

She was sleeping, no, not asleep, but her eyes were closed, she was lying on a couch. Someone spoke, a man she could not see.

"If you'd worn the topaz," he said, "nothing could have happened to you. You're to blame, you knew better, why did you let the brooch out of your hands?"

"But I didn't," she protested to the doctor. Yes, he was a doctor, the unseen man — a psychiatrist. When she realized this she began to be afraid. "I have the brooch right here," she said.

"Look again. *She* wore it, the other, pinned over her heart. And she died." His voice was accusing.

"No, no," she cried wildly and tried to sit up, but her eyes would not open, she could not move. "It isn't my fault." But when she curved her fingers into her palms, both hands were empty.

The doctor's voice changed, became gruff. "Go back, go back, there's no way out except through the past. You can't go anywhere but back . . ."

Kitty found herself standing in the opened front door, Blue pressed against her, barking and wagging his tail, delighted with her company. She shook her head, confused. I must have walked in my sleep, she thought. Otherwise how did I get here? I was dreaming and I walked in my sleep like I used to when I was little. A shock went through her. And I remembered something, she told herself. But nothing more came.

She patted the dog, calmed him, and then brought him into her bedroom. "You wake me up if I start that kind of thing again," she told him.

She got back into bed, checked under her pillow — yes, the brooch was still there. Had the dream meant anything? She had thought of a psychiatrist just before she went to sleep. Likely that was what caused the dream. It's all right now, Blue's here, and the topaz . . .

Someone called her name and she rose from a sanctuary, rose to the perilous surface.

"Kitty."

She opened her eyes. The room was bright with daylight, Rhoddie stood beside the bed. "Old Blue really enjoyed himself — in all night. When did you let him in?"

"Oh, sometime." Kitty yawned, stretched.

"It's getting late," Rhoddie said. "I've got an appointment at Sharp Hospital this morning and I don't want to go alone."

"But I — I was thinking about buying a suitcase and I . . ." Kitty sat up.

"So, okay. If you're determined to leave, we'll shop for suitcases after I get through at Sharp. We'll come back and eat lunch and then go shopping."

"But I . . ."

"I don't want to go to the hospital alone and I told Gill to get lost, so he took off with that bunch that wants to start a combo."

"All right," Kitty said. "I'll hurry."

She showered and dressed in her best pantsuit. She would be traveling later today. Somewhere. She pinned the topaz brooch on the shirt, considered the effect, then took it off and put it in the pocket of the jacket that went with the pants.

She went into the kitchen. "Why are you going to the hospital?" she asked Rhoddie.

Rhoddie waved her decorated cast in the air. "They're going to take another X-ray. Who knows, maybe they'll chop the thing off."

"Rhoddie," Kitty said, "I'm going to leave. You know that."

"Let's talk about it later."

"I can't wait. I should have found another place to live a long time ago." Kitty held up her hand as Rhoddie started to protest. "No, I mean what I say. Three doesn't work out. You and Gill, you'd be fine alone together. I'm the extra."

"You never were extra."

Kitty smiled at the vehement tone. Rhoddie wouldn't admit to the problems of two women and one man living in the same house.

"Gill taking that money . . ." Rhoddie sighed. "I don't know if I can ever forgive him. To think he'd want to hurt you in any way. I just can't believe it."

"If I leave town everything will quiet down. This — this man, whoever he is, can't watch me all the time, I'll make sure no one follows me when I leave."

"But where will you go?"

"I don't know yet," Kitty said. "I must get away from San Diego."

"I have a friend in Frisco. Maybe . . ."

"No," Kitty said quickly. "I'll have to stay away from people you know, I might be traced. But San Francisco is an idea . . ."

"Hey, look at the time. I'm going to miss my appointment," Rhoddie said. "We've got to hurry."

Rhoddie drove, the cast on her left arm making her awkward. Kitty felt ashamed of her own refusal to drive. I know the mechanics, she thought, I stamp on an imaginary brake when Gill takes his time in slowing down, but I just

162

can't get behind the wheel. I can't. Her heart began to beat faster thinking about driving a car herself. Blue thrust his cold nose into her neck and she jumped.

"I can take the dog for a walk while you're in the hospital," she said to Rhoddie.

"That's not why I wanted you to come — I need moral support. I've always been a big baby about getting hurt. You don't know how I felt last Thursday when no one could find you and Gill wasn't there either. I tell you, I climbed the walls. They had to give me a shot to knock me out."

Kitty could not refuse Rhoddie, but after they pulled into the parking lot and got out of the van her steps lagged.

"Hurry up, we're late."

In through the entrance, down one corridor, then another. Kitty felt as though she had entered a maze by the time they found the X-ray department. RADIOLOGY, the sign said.

I don't like being inside this hospital, Kitty thought. No wonder I didn't stay last Thursday if I felt the way I do now. What did I do then? Wherever the emergency room is, that's where they brought us, Rhoddie said. Did I climb off a stretcher and run out the door? There should be a memory, something, but there was nothing.

"Look at that line," Rhoddie said. "I might have known I didn't need to worry about being on time, I have to wait anyway."

Other people with casts sat in chairs. No one

looked directly at anyone else. "Why is it you always have to wait for doctors," Rhoddie said. "Is that what they teach at medical school — how to make people wait?"

Some of the others stared at Rhoddie. A girl giggled.

"I'm nervous," Rhoddie said, "and it makes me hungry. Wasn't there candy in those machines we passed?"

"I don't know. I guess so."

"Why don't you go find out. I need a candy bar and I don't want to lose my turn." She dumped coins in Kitty's hand.

Kitty wandered through the corridors, more than ever feeling she was lost in a maze. Surely she should see the machines soon. A man in a wheelchair went past her. I'll ask him, she thought, but before she could form the question he spoke.

"You know where the pay phone is?" he asked.

"No, sorry, I don't."

He went on, not waiting, and she shrugged.

All this white, Kitty thought. Why must nurses wear white, someone told me once that white, not black, was the color of death. Who? Who told me? Not Rhoddie or Gill.

A man passed wearing a green pajama-like outfit. A surgeon? she wondered. On TV they had caps covering their hair, and masks. All green. Why? So the patient in the operating room wouldn't look at white and decide it was time to die?

164

I'm frightened, she thought. I'm thinking all these things to keep myself from running out of here. What's wrong with me? This is a hospital, but hospitals aren't that bad. It's me, this hospital scares me. I have to find the machine fast and get back to Rhoddie, she thought, or I won't go back at all. Maybe I can't find my way back anyway, maybe I'll wander around these halls forever, lost . . . Oh, stop! she admonished herself.

A voice spoke to her left, calling a girl's name. She half turned her head, caught a glimpse of a brown-haired man but kept walking, he was a stranger and the name he called was not hers.

"Risa. Please wait, Risa. It's Jim. Jim Halloway."

The brown-haired man was touching her, holding her arm. She tried to draw away.

"Risa. Don't be afraid."

"I — I think you've made a mistake," she said. "My name isn't Risa."

He stared at her. He was so close she could see the pupils of his hazel eyes widen. A nice-looking man but she didn't know him.

Wait — Gill had mentioned a doctor, said she had gone off in a car with a doctor. She could not remember the name Gill had told her. Dr. Halloway?

"Don't be frightened of me," the man said.

"I — I'm not." But she was. "Are you a doctor?" she asked.

"Yes. You don't remember?"

She shook her head.

"You don't know me at all?" The even quality of his voice changed, roughened.

He's upset, Kitty thought.

"I know you as Risa," he said. "Risa Mac-Arthur."

"I'm Kitty," she said and then stopped. Should she tell him anything? A strong sense of danger pervaded her. She was afraid of this doctor who said he knew her, who Gill insisted had driven her to Del Mar last Thursday. Had he shared any more of the missing time with her? What had they done? She bit her lip, glanced to one side, then the other.

"Kitty?" he repeated. "Kitty what?" His voice was low and gentle again.

She wouldn't tell him. She could feel tension rising in her until it seemed the top of her head would crack from the pressure. Her head would split and all the lost memories would tumble out for everyone to see and then, and then . . .

Kitty jerked free of Dr. Halloway's grasp and began running, turning corners at random. She passed the entrance to Radiology, kept going. Rhoddie couldn't help, no one could help. Must get away, run, danger, danger . . .

At last she pushed through doors that led outside. She was in the parking lot. Where was the gray van? She saw it, hurried down the rows of parked cars. She would take Blue, they'd find a pay phone, call Rhoddie in X-ray and tell her where they were, she could come and get them when she finished. Then when they were all safely home she would pack and leave, right away. She would leave now but the money was still in the bank, she needed money . . .

She was brought up short when a hand grasped her arm.

"No," she said without looking. "No, no, I'm not Risa. Let me go, let me go." She jerked and twisted her arm but couldn't get away.

Then she was whirled about, arms held her close, her face pressed into a man's chest, a corduroy jacket.

"Stop that," a voice said, not the man's voice she had heard in the hospital, not the doctor's voice. "Look at me."

She pulled back, straining away from this new peril, stared into a tanned face, brown — no, coppery — eyes. Copper-colored hair spilled down over the jacket collar. He was the handsomest man she had ever seen.

"Risa," he repeated. "Stop being foolish."

"I'm not . . ." she began, but a thrill of recognition shot through her, a name rose from somewhere deep inside.

"Rory," she said.

❧ *16* ❧

"You do know me." Rory's voice was light, confident. "I thought you would." He leaned over, touched her lips lightly with his. She shivered. "Risa?" he asked.

Her mind whirled. Risa? Yes, yes, she was, of course she was Risa. And yet, and yet . . . Faces, names swirled about almost within reach. Rhoddie? Where was Rhoddie? Then the thought slipped away.

She was Risa MacArthur. But hadn't she just denied it? Why? There was no time to think with Rory here holding her. Rory. "I've kept looking for you," she said.

He released her but kept her hand. "The car's this way," he said, pulling her with him.

Risa didn't see the copper Ferrari anywhere. Copper? Doubt clouded her mind. Rory's Ferrari was copper colored to match his copper hair, his eyes, a beautiful car like its owner. And yet the idea of the Ferrari in this parking lot seemed wrong. She turned to Rory and he smiled, teeth white against his tan.

"Glad to see me?"

"Oh, Rory, I've been so . . ." So what? Confused, yes. Where were they anyway? What was this parking lot, that tall white building? Something clicked in her mind. Sharp Hospital. And she had come here with someone, come for a reason she couldn't quite find.

They passed a van and a dog barked furiously from inside, the van rocking with his efforts to burst from it. A black dog. There was something about a black dog and she hesitated, but Rory pulled her along.

"Here's my new car," he said, opening the door for her to get in. Gold, a shiny metallic gold. Not copper, why had she thought . . . "What make?" Risa asked.

"Jaguar. You like?"

"I like," she answered.

She watched Rory slide behind the wheel. She decided he looked older, strained. Was he ill? Is that why they had been at the hospital? No — no, she had met Rory after she came out of the hospital, she had been running, hadn't expected to see him. Why had she run? What from? "You know, I have a headache," she said.

"We'll get some aspirin when we stop."

"There's some at home." Home, I'm going home with Rory, she thought. Everything is all right. But a name edged into her mind. Allegra. Allegra? The face came next, long blond hair, brilliant sapphire eyes, beautiful. I know her. I even recall not liking her, why don't I know who she is, where she belongs? Allegra. What is her last name? Did I go to Sharp Hospital with her?

The green freeway signs flashed by. Rory passed the Del Mar turnoff and kept on going toward Los Angeles.

"Aren't we going home?"

"No. A little surprise. I remember how you like surprises and I've been promising you one for a long time." His voice was strained too.

I ought to feel something more, some response, Risa thought. This is Rory, I'm with Rory, with the man I love more than anything else in the world. But her head hurt, the throbbing made her thoughts more chaotic than before.

"I — I'm all mixed-up," she said.

His head turned to look at her. "You've got circles under your eyes. Why don't you take a little nap. We'll be awhile getting where we're going."

Obediently Risa leaned her head back and closed her eyes. She was tired, maybe that was why her mind was so disordered, why she could not find information, facts. Everything was all right, she was in the Ferrari with — No, not the Ferrari, this was the new car. Had he sold the Ferrari? She couldn't remember.

She did remember going down to Baja in the Ferrari, she and Rory. They had gone down as far as Ensenada, where he kept his boat when it was not moored in San Diego. She was supposed to drive the car back while he sailed the boat on to San Diego, despite the fact she did not drive all that well and hated to drive alone, especially in Mexico. Of course, Rory had asked her and she would do anything for him. But she really hated driving by herself in Mexico.

Another name, another face drifted across her

mind. A girl, long dark hair braided down her back, dirty cutoff jeans, bare feet, and a ragged blood-spattered T-shirt. Katrinka Morgan. "For God's sake call me Kitty, can you imagine the mentality of parents who would name a helpless baby Katrinka?"

This was in the motel, though, after Risa had taken her there. This was after the nosebleed had stopped, after Kitty had taken a shower. They had thrown Kitty's clothes away and she dressed in a pair of Risa's jeans and a pullover sweater Rory had given Risa for her birthday.

I hated to give up that sweater, Risa thought, but Kitty was a taker, she took whatever appealed to her. I hope Rory never finds out about the sweater. She almost opened her eyes to glance guiltily at him beside her in the driver's seat.

He would have been furious if he had known Risa picked up a strange girl on the road. He never picked up hitchhikers.

But there were quite a few things Rory did not know. First of all, Risa had gone back to the motel after she'd seen Rory off on the boat. She had taken the motel key with her by mistake and wanted to bring it back. Of course, she hadn't mentioned this to Rory — he complained about her inefficiency anyway. On the way back she had seen this girl walking, head down, stumbling in the dirt along the road, and Risa had wondered if she was sick and had looked at her with more concern and then seen the bloodstained T-shirt and stopped the Ferrari without thinking.

I should have known the brakes were bad then, Risa said to herself. The car pulled to the right and was hard to stop. I should have known. Then again at the motel the Ferrari acted funny but I was worried about the girl and her nosebleed, seemed as though the blood would never stop, but the cold washcloth helped. Then what could I do? Kitty Morgan needed a ride to Los Angeles, I wasn't going to L.A. but could take her to San Diego, maybe see she got money to go on. Oh, I know I could have given her money right then and let her take a bus all the way, but I hated to drive alone and she needed a ride. Rory wouldn't know, he was on the boat, what he didn't know he couldn't get angry about.

The only trouble was Risa didn't like Kitty. The dirty, bleeding girl on the road was one person whereas the girl who sat in the passenger seat with her while she drove along the Mexican roads toward San Diego seemed totally different.

"You sure must have the bread. Been running stuff over the border? Got some stashed in the car now?"

"What do you mean?"

"Okay, you're not going to admit anything, I wouldn't either." Kitty shrugged, began to fiddle with the radio. "That's a neat pin you're wearing. Let me see it."

Without asking, Kitty unpinned the topaz brooch from the shirt Risa wore and held the stone in her hands. Risa almost stopped the car then and there to snatch the topaz away, so acutely did she feel the violation. "Please give it back to me," she managed to say. "The brooch is a gift from my mother."

But Kitty laughed and calmly pinned the brooch on her sweater, on the sweater Risa had lent her. "Oh, let me wear it for a while — what difference does it make?"

All the difference in the world. Risa's throat tightened, her vision blurred at the edges. For a moment she thought she would black out and she took several deep breaths, focusing on the road. She certainly did not want any accidents while she was driving Rory's Ferrari — he would never forgive her. She glanced at the darkening sky and saw she wouldn't get to Tijuana before night fell.

The topaz was hers, not Kitty Morgan's. Rory had given the brooch to her only the night before, almost like an engagement present, but of course it was not really from Rory. And they were not engaged.

They had eaten in the Ensenada restaurant Rory liked best, she'd had margueritas as she always did in Mexico. Rory was drinking vodka on the rocks as he always did, Mexico or anyplace, he had had quite a few, he stumbled on the crushed shells outside the restaurant on their way to the car. She had caught his arm and he lurched against her.

"Pretty little thing," he told her, words running together. "All grown up now." He caught her in his arms and kissed her, holding her so close she couldn't breathe. There was a sudden sharp pain above her left breast and it was a few seconds before she realized something in his shirt pocket was jabbing into her, hurting her.

"Ouch," she gasped and struggled away from him. "You've got something sharp in your pocket. What is it?" She reached up and felt inside the pocket and then the topaz brooch was in her hand.

"Oh," she exclaimed. "Oh, Rory, is this for me?"

"What?"

"This jewel. It feels warm, it feels familiar, like I've . . ." Her words trailed off. She did not remember seeing the gem before but yet it was familiar in a way she couldn't understand.

"That's a topaz brooch," Rory said. His words were no longer blurred, he had straightened, looked more alert. "Maybe you saw the thing as a child because I got it out of your aunt's safety deposit box." He fumbled in his shirt pocket. "This was wrapped around the brooch." He handed her a crumpled piece of paper and she moved closer to the neon light of the restaurant and read:

"Marie — This is for Risa, keep it safe for her. Merry."

My mother, Risa thought. Why didn't Aunt Marie give me the brooch? Did she ever plan to? Was it one more thing to withhold like she with-

174

held my father's identity all these years? Risa stared into the golden brown of the topaz and smiled. My mother left this for me, she loved me.

"I would have let you have it earlier," Rory said, "but the pin of the brooch is crooked and I thought I'd have a new one . . ."

"No," Risa interrupted. "I want it left this way." Her fingers curved protectively around the gem.

Rory shrugged. He seemed to be completely sober. "There were a few papers, like I told you, in the box too. Nothing important, but if you want to see them . . ."

Risa shook her head. "You know more about that than I do. You take care of them."

"She shouldn't have left everything to me," he said.

Risa laughed. "What little there was. And that was your father's to begin with. Aunt Marie had nothing of her own except the ranch — we were always poor. Oh, Rory, what would I do without you?"

He looked at her a long time without speaking. His face was bleak. Finally he seemed to shake himself and grinned at her. "Just because I've made out my will in your favor doesn't mean there'll be anything left for you when I'm gone."

Don't talk about dying, she wanted to cry. I can't bear to think you'll ever leave me. But she smiled and said, "What do you think you'll get from me? My will may leave everything to you but that's a big fat goose egg."

"Ah, but now you have the topaz," he had pointed out. "If you'd like me to try and sell it for you I think it's worth quite a bit."

"No!" Her voice had been indignant. "It's mine."

Not Kitty Morgan's, she had no right to sit there with the topaz pinned over her heart, investigating all the pockets and compartments of Rory's car, none of her business.

"Hey, here's something I found stuck in the bottom," Kitty said. "Wow! If I looked like this I sure as hell wouldn't be hitchhiking back to L.A." She held a photograph out to Risa, then snatched it back to examine it again. "You know her? Or the guy? He's some foxy dude, I should be so lucky."

The picture was creased but Risa had recognized Rory immediately. She had never seen the girl he was standing next to, arm around her, holding her close. A blonde, very pretty. No one she knew, she thought she'd seen all of Rory's old girlfriends. Was this someone new? How could she compete with a woman so much prettier?

"He your boyfriend?" Kitty asked.

Risa shook her head. Not really. And yet he had been different lately, since Aunt Marie died. He seemed to worry about her, had even insisted they make out wills in each other's favor so she would have some protection if anything happened to him. She had nothing to leave him except the topaz.

"Kitty, please give me back the brooch. I don't like to have anyone else wear it."

But Kitty was still engrossed in the picture. "Hey, you know, I'll bet this is a wedding picture, she's got a corsage and isn't that a church in the background?"

"Don't be silly," Risa snapped. "And I want that brooch now."

Kitty let the picture slip from her hands. "How much is it worth?" she asked.

Risa took a deep breath. "I don't know."

"What kind of stone is it?"

"A topaz."

"Hey, that's November. I'm a Moon Child, some still say Cancer for my zodiac sign but I like Moon Child better. You're a Scorpio, I guess. When's your birthday?"

"November twentieth."

"Then the topaz is your birthstone. What's the matter, you think it's unlucky for another sign to be wearing your birthstone?"

"I just want it back." Risa's hands were clutching the wheel in annoyance and unease. The feeling that something was wrong grew within her until she felt like screaming aloud.

"Hey, you're really uptight about this," Kitty laughed. "I always seem to pick the weirdos. Okay, here's . . ."

Kitty never finished the sentence. The Ferrari had been climbing the hill by Salsipuedes, up and up and around, and then Risa started down, found she was going a little too fast and put her

177

foot on the brake. The car pulled to the right and something gave, Risa could feel it go and then there were no brakes, the car slewed as she tried to bring it back on the road, she was going too fast, much too fast, and she could not control where she was headed and the rocks were there, they were going to crash and she took her hands from the steering wheel to put them up before her face and someone was screaming, was it Kitty? Then the Ferrari was rolling sideways, a blur of motion and she was falling, falling, and her head struck against something and she knew nothing more.

17

"No, no," Risa moaned, reaching out. She touched an arm, grasped it, opened her eyes. "Oh, Rory, I remembered the accident." Despite the fact she knew herself to be with Rory now, in another car entirely, in another place, the terror of that earlier time clung to her. Her breath came in short painful gasps, she trembled, holding to Rory's arm.

"What did happen?" he asked.

"I — There was another girl," she stammered.

"I know that," he said. "After all, I buried someone, thinking she was you."

"But we — we weren't alike. How could you . . . ?"

His face was turned from her and she saw a muscle twitch in his cheek. "She was battered, unrecognizable." His voice was flat, unemotional. "She wore your clothes, the sweater I'd given you. I thought you'd been alone in the Ferrari. Of course I thought she was you."

"But her hair wasn't curly, it was dark, like mine, but . . ."

He did turn to her then. "Risa, I didn't look at the body any longer than I had to. Can't you understand? I thought it was you, I was upset."

"Then when did you know I was alive?"

He was silent a moment. "Allegra told me," he

said finally. "But by then you'd disappeared. I've searched for you everywhere."

Allegra. The name was back, the picture in her mind, the snapshot Kitty held in the Ferrari. Allegra. In the house at Del Mar, in Rory's house. Rory's fiancée, the emerald ring. "You're going to marry her," Risa said. She took her hand from his arm.

He said nothing.

"You've known her a long time. Since before the accident. You — you hid her from me."

"Oh, come on, Risa, since when have I shared my entire life with you?"

"But . . ." She wanted to say this was different, she had believed he loved her, Risa, and all the time Allegra had been there in the background.

Hadn't he told her . . . ? No, he never had, not really, never said he loved her. Other words, words she had taken to mean love. Allegra's face came to her again, the sparkling eyes, the shimmer of her blond hair, the high tinkly laugh. Allegra, who probably had always collected men like coins, keeping them only if they had value. Rory. And Jim.

Risa sat up straight, fire shooting along her nerves. Jim. Jim Halloway, she had just seen Jim. Where? And she hadn't — what hadn't she done? Something was wrong, she had done a terrible thing, how could she have forgotten Jim?

"Rory, I've got to make a phone call."

"Who to?"

She was silent, Jim's name trembling on her

lips. How could she explain to Rory? "You — you know I lost some of my memories for a while," she said at last. She distrusted the word amnesia, disliked using it.

"I hoped that was the case. I'd hate to think you've been hiding from me."

She stared at him in amazement. "Hide from you? Why would I? I've been looking for you. I thought Allegra was . . ." She shrugged. "Well, I guess I was being silly. But someone did help me when I was so — so lost. A doctor. And when I was at the hospital, just before you found me, I — someway I didn't recognize him when he spoke to me, told him I wasn't Risa. I must call him, I don't know what he thinks of me acting like that."

Rory touched her arm, ran his fingers down to hold her hand. "Can't we have a few hours alone without another man intruding?"

Risa glanced at him, he was looking at her and smiling.

"After all, Risa, it's been over a year since we've been together."

A year, yes, the accident was in another November. Her head began to throb painfully again, she put her free hand up to her forehead. "I'm still confused," she said.

Rory took his hand away. "Rest. You need to recuperate."

Her eyes seemed to close by themselves, shutting out the sunlight that seared her head, shutting out what was now. I want to sleep, she thought, sleep and wake up and have everything in the right compartments in my mind, have everything like it used to be.

But Kitty Morgan's face was waiting for her, the girl's screams echoing in her ears. Once again she relived the Ferrari's smash into the rocks, going over the edge, her own fall into space, the blackness. Then the painful awakening on the rocks, the confusion. In the dusk, everything was shadow and all she could remember was the topaz, she didn't have the topaz brooch, someone else was wearing the gem, it belonged to her, not to the other. She must find the topaz.

Her head hurt and she was dizzy so she had to crawl, sliding from one rock to another, going down to where the last red rays of the setting sun showed her a lightness against the rocks.

Darkness came, blending with the shadows between the rocks, but she persisted and at last her fingers touched softness, a sticky wetness. She concentrated on the topaz, shutting away the messages her hands transmitted. This was the other, the one who pinned the topaz on the sweater. Feel the wool of the sweater, so sticky, never mind, here's the pin, unfasten the pin, take the brooch in your hand, don't mind the stickiness, don't think what it might be, you have the topaz, close your hand tight and get away. No, don't sink down into blackness, there's danger, something terrible is here, death is here. You must get away, crawl over the rocks, slide down to the bottom, there has to be an end to the descending.

Yes, now the sand of the beach is gritty, taking away the horrible feel in your hands, they're gritty, sandy. Keep the topaz safe, stand up, yes, you can stand, lean against the rock, wait a moment. No, don't think. Not safe to think. Safety is in moving, getting away, holding the topaz, the topaz will take you to safety.

But words in her head made her stop her lurching progress down the beach. "Kitty," the voice said in her brain, "Kitty Morgan." The words were etched in red letters across her mind. She had emptied her head of all thoughts, but the words stuck there, indelible. She slipped sideways, fell into a crevice between the rocks and was unable to urge her body to further movement. "Kitty," her brain flashed in red, and then there was blackness.

Noise, a dog barking, wetness on her face, hands puffing at her, carrying her, a light, painful and blinding, the cold *snick snick* of scissors. Her head hurt, voices probed at her and she couldn't answer.

"What's your name? What happened? Can you talk?"

The questions resounded in the emptiness of her mind and she made an effort. "Kitty," she said. "Kitty Morgan."

"What did you say?" a man's voice asked.

Risa struggled into awareness. Rory. She was

driving in this new gold car with Rory. Kitty Morgan belonged in the then. This was now, she was Risa. But she had been Kitty. How could she have been Kitty when Kitty was another girl and Kitty was dead?

"You said Kitty Morgan." Rory's voice was harsh.

"She was the — the girl. The one you buried. But I . . ." Risa paused, slipped her hand into the pocket of her jacket. Yes, the topaz was with her, safe, along with the coins Rhoddie had given her for the candy machine. Rhoddie.

They had picked her up on the beach, mind-less. Rhoddie and Gill and Blue. Blue, the big black dog. That was what she tried to remember in the parking lot outside of Sharp Hospital a while ago. It had been Blue barking so furiously, yes, in the gray van, she recalled the van. And Rhoddie. She had left poor Rhoddie alone. Again.

"Rory, I have to get to a phone. I've done a terrible thing."

"What did you do?"

"I left my friend at Sharp Hospital and she doesn't know where I've gone, what happened to me. She — she doesn't even know my name, not my real name."

"What are you talking about?"

"Oh, Rory, I've been somebody else for a whole year. I've been Kitty Morgan. No wonder you couldn't find me. I didn't remember anything, not you or the house at Del Mar. I didn't even know who I was. All I had was the topaz." And Kitty's name, she thought. I took the topaz from her dead body and took her name too. Rory said she was so battered she couldn't be recognized. Risa recalled the feel of soft stickiness on her fingers and shuddered.

"You remember being Kitty Morgan." His inflection made it a statement, not a question.

Why does he sound so strained? she wondered. "Can't we stop soon?" she asked. "I want to call Rhoddie." Jim too, but better not mention that again.

"I want you to myself for the rest of the day," Rory said. "I don't want to share you with any of these strangers you've accumulated in the year away from me. Is that too much to ask?"

"But I only want to make a phone call so she won't worry . . ."

"No."

Risa sat back in her seat hurt and angry. Typical of Rory, arrogant, only considering what he wanted. Selfish. Aunt Marie had always said so. "Charming and I'm fond of him, but don't expect him to think of anyone but Rory." Well, he had to stop for gas sometime. She would find a phone then.

"Where are we going?" She tried to make her voice pleasant, conciliatory.

"I told you I wanted to surprise you. I've been planning for this ever since I knew you weren't dead after all."

His words seemed to hang in the air, waiting

for her to grasp the meaning. She turned to him and he was smiling at her. She smiled back, her headache was better, what was wrong with her that she could not relax and enjoy being with Rory?

She wouldn't close her eyes and dredge up any more memories of the lost year. Everything she remembered drove a wedge between her and Rory. She wanted to anticipate the surprise with interest and pleasure but all she could think of was Rhoddie frantic with worry. And Jim — No, best not to think of Jim at all, there was something there she didn't want to examine, not now. Not here with Rory.

Risa watched for the green freeway signs. Bakersfield? Were they headed for the San Joaquin Valley? For the ranch? Misgivings crept through her.

"We're going to the ranch, aren't we?"

"Yes. You've guessed that much, I knew you would, but the surprise is something else. You'll have to wait and see."

"I didn't realize you knew how to get to the ranch."

"You talked of it so much, told me what you remembered of your childhood there, that I feel I know the place. Don't you recall how you chattered on and on about living there?"

"Yes, and bored you stiff. I never would have suspected you really listened to me."

"I don't miss much."

There was no reason to be nervous because

they were going to the ranch, there was nothing to be afraid of at the ranch. Then why was she so uncomfortable? She had been there with Jim and Allegra. When? She searched for the date. Sunday. Jim had the weekend off and Allegra had invited herself. Had she told Rory?

"What does Allegra think of you taking me off like this?" she asked.

"Why should she know?"

"Then it's a secret from everyone?"

She watched him turn toward her, watched him smile with his white teeth dramatic against his tanned face. But his eyes had a flat metallic look.

"I don't know if I want to go," she said. "The ranch is dead, the house, the fields. There's only the weeds now."

"But you are going, just the same," he said, and the metal was in his voice now. He swerved onto an off-ramp, drove into a gas station.

She reached for the door handle.

"Where are you going?"

"To — Well, I have to use the ladies' room," she said. She was going to make the phone calls no matter what Rory wanted. She could call Rhoddie collect at home, she must be home by now.

But Rory got out of the car, too, and walked with her to the bathroom. "I think the men's is on the other side," she said, but he was waiting when she came out.

"Look, Rory, I'm going to call Rhoddie.

187

What's wrong with that?"

He grasped her arm, so hard she cried out. "I told you no. No phone calls. Now get back in the car and stop trying to lie to me."

She thought of screaming, of calling out to the attendant, but what could she say? I want to make a phone call and he won't let me? Rory could be so unreasonable. She took her place in the passenger's seat, stiff with annoyance.

How could I ever have thought he was so wonderful, forgotten his dominance of me, his insistence I do everything exactly as he wanted? Scenes blazed up in her mind, humiliations inflicted on her in front of others and her blind disregard of everything but her need to be with Rory. Why?

"You never loved me," she said. "You never will."

He said nothing but reached over and put his hand on her nape, began caressing her skin. Shivers coursed through her, the familiar sensation of drowning in Rory's touch, but her mind sent up a flare.

He's doing this deliberately. He knows how he can make me feel and yet he feels nothing. She jerked away from his touch.

They drove on in silence. She put her hand in her jacket pocket and touched the topaz brooch for reassurance. It was warm in her fingers. A topaz for my Lady Fair . . .

Jim. Jim had said the words to her. Jim had held her close and she had thrust him away. How could she have forgotten him for even a moment? Jim saying the words her great-great-grandfather had written to her great-great-grandmother.

Another line from the poem came back to her: "To keep her safe from violent harm . . ."

❧ 18 ❧

"Rory, I want to go home."

"But you are. Isn't the ranch your real home? Remember how you used to go on about the place as though it was a never-never land."

"I was a child then. Be reasonable, Rory. Let's go back to Del Mar. It's getting late, we won't have time for a picnic at the ranch, or whatever it is that you've planned."

"There'll be time."

"Please. I — I don't feel right, my head hurts . . ."

"Stop talking then and close your eyes," he said. "Go to sleep."

Jim, she thought, I wish you were with me now instead of Rory. I would never run away from you again like I did in the hospital, like I did in Ensenada . . .

Risa stared unseeing out the windshield at the late afternoon sky. Now she remembered the night in Jim's apartment when Mac had talked to her, saw in her mind the distorted memory that had frightened her then. She had seen Kitty, blood spattered and wearing the topaz, and panic had closed her mind, caused her to be terrified of the psychiatrist.

So she had fled to the beach at Salsipuedes, following some unconscious urging. She had climbed down the rocks, perhaps the same rocks where the Ferrari had crashed, where she'd crawled to the dead Kitty Morgan in the night and taken back the topaz brooch and forgotten Risa MacArthur and all of Risa's memories.

But now all the memories were merging together. On the rocks at Salsipuedes she had stood in the sunset and felt the fear of a year before, a fear she could now understand. But wait — No, not just that. Someone had come, someone was above her on the rocks, a danger whispering her name. An unseen menace like the night at The Copper King. Who followed her, wanted her dead? She was a threat to no one. The memories were back, most of them, and nowhere could she see a reason for someone to try to kill her.

Jim had followed her to Baja, rescued her from the rocks, frightening away the pursuer. Jim had saved her from falling into the old well at the ranch. Oh, Jim, she thought, how can I ever explain to you how I woke in the night in that Ensenada motel and didn't know I was Risa, didn't know you were next door? How can you ever forgive me for not remembering your smile, your touch . . . ?

Suddenly she was furious at Rory. If Blue was here. I wish I had Blue here, he'd show Rory. It was Rory he was barking at in the parking lot, Rory who was taking me away. They all must think I've lost my mind, running off once, twice. I wish I'd stopped to tell Rhoddie I was leaving.

No one knows where I am.

Rory pulled onto the turnoff for Porterville.

At least we're almost there, it's almost over, whatever surprise he's planned. Then we can go back to Del Mar and then . . . Why, I'll leave, she thought. I don't want to live in that house anymore, not with Rory or even without him. He's welcome to Allegra and she to him.

It was as though chains had dropped away. I'm free, she said to herself, I don't love him, it was the love of a worshiper for a self-created idol. Rory wasn't ever what I told myself he was, not a god, just a man and a rather nasty one to boot. I don't even like him very well.

I can find a place to live, not with Rhoddie and Gill, she'll always be my friend but I won't need constant support, I can stand on my own, I have a job. I'm Topaz, she thought, and smiled. I wonder if Jim will like Topaz?

"Feeling better?" Rory asked.

"Quite a lot better," she said.

Rhoddie would be so surprised when she heard the whole story. Even Gill would raise his eyebrows. Has he found the red-haired man, I wonder, the one in the gold sports car who caused the accident in the van, who forced us off the road? Gold. Risa had a moment when her mind stopped functioning. Then impressions, ideas, realizations began to flood her head until she felt she was drowning. Rory. His hair is copper, Gill would say red, the car is gold, a gold-colored Jaguar. Jim saw a gold sports car in

Baja. Rory. Rory wants me dead. Why? Why? And then, with a thrill of horror: he's taking me to the ranch to kill me.

Risa sat as still as she could, afraid to turn her head, afraid to swallow, lest the motion in some way let Rory know she was aware of the nature of his surprise. How could he call it that, remembering her delight in surprises as a child, how could he?

I've got to get away. But the car was traveling far too fast for her to try to jump from it. That was sure death. When he stops, she decided, no matter where, I'll get out and run.

But the road bypassed Porterville and there were no stop signs. She saw the twisted oak, the Indian reservation sign, and the tree farm with disbelief. Not so soon. Here was the access road to the ranch and still she had not had a chance. Maybe if she set herself to leap out when he slowed for the stop . . .

In one motion Rory slammed the car to a stop and grabbed her arm. "You've sat like a zombie the last hour. You've caught on, haven't you?"

She tried to turn her face to him, to smile, to pretend, but she was too frightened.

"Come on." He yanked her over the shift lever, opened his door, and forced her to squirm under the steering wheel and out his side too. He twisted her arm up behind her back, not hurting but uncomfortable. She had a sudden clear recollection of the time at the beach when he had slapped her because she'd gone surfing with one of his friends after Rory had told her to bug off and stop bothering them. She remembered crying, sobbing out that his friend had asked her, she hadn't been a pest, not really. Rory's words came back to her clearly. "It makes no difference — you didn't do what I said. Now maybe you've learned a lesson." How could she have adored him all these years, been so blind?

"Why, Rory?" she asked, her voice husky. "You don't have any reason."

"The will," he said. "You left me everything in your will."

"But I . . ." she began and cut off her words with a gasp when he increased the pressure on her arm.

"Shut up," he said. "I'm talking."

Tears rolled down her cheeks from the pain in her arm.

"You didn't die in the accident," Rory went on. "I tried, I lost a beautiful car there for nothing. You didn't die. What was I to do, I couldn't explain the other girl so I said she was you and buried her. But I knew damn well you were alive somewhere, you dressed someone else in your clothes and she died — but where the hell were you?"

"The accident," Risa said after a moment. "You arranged it? But I still don't — I mean I don't have anything. Just the topaz, no money at all. What good is the will?"

"You always got in the way," he said. "I didn't mean for you to have the brooch either. I took the topaz down to Mexico to sell it to a guy I know and you had to find the thing and babble about how you recognized the stone and so I had to give it to you."

Not even the topaz, Risa thought. He didn't even mean to give me that. "Something else must have been in the safety deposit box," she said. "I can't imagine what — Aunt Marie had no money, no stocks. You found something, though, didn't you?"

"A quarter of a million dollars," he said.

"I don't believe you," Risa said. "Anyway, Aunt Marie's will left everything to you, even the ranch. What have I got to do with the money?"

"It's yours. The money was always yours, all your life. Now I know why my father married your aunt. I thought he was crazy marrying that dried-up old spinster, he always had an eye for a pretty girl, and your aunt . . . If he hadn't had his heart attack so soon after the wedding he'd have gotten the money someway, I know my father. But he didn't tell me, I never knew."

"I don't understand," she whispered.

"Your father. Your dear dead father that Aunt Marie was so careful never to mention, your father left you the money. Only one hundred thousand to begin with, but she never touched any of it except when she asked my father to set up a way that income tax could be paid from it. That's how he knew the money was there, he was a tax lawyer and she heard about him from someone and wrote him a letter . . ."

195

"My — my father?" Risa stammered. "The money came from him?"

"God knows why Marie let it lie there in the bank," Rory said. "I suppose she had one of her weird ideas about tainted money and couldn't bear to think you might be contaminated by it. But the money was — is — in your name, and there in the safety deposit box were all the interest statements, the original savings book, everything. All addressed to you."

"My father." Risa began to cry.

"Well, if my father hadn't died, he'd have convinced your crazy aunt to declare herself your guardian and use the money, get control. After all, you were a minor then. But he died and I didn't know. Not until she died too."

"But I — I would have shared . . ."

"With me? How about Allegra too?" Rory laughed. "She's my wife, you know. We married in a fit of misunderstanding when we both thought the other had money."

"But you do. The house, the boat . . ."

"The house has been refinanced. I won't be able to keep it without your money. The boat — it's gone. And the car isn't paid for. There isn't any money, Risa, why did you think there was?" His voice was mocking. "There's never been enough. My father was a lousy investor, he left very little. Marie squeezed each buck but even then it didn't last. That's why I need yours. I might have married you but Allegra was already my wife by the time your aunt died and I found the money existed."

It all seemed completely unreal to Risa. She had to remind herself this was Rory holding her in front of him, telling her this fantastic story about money, almost caressingly into her ear. Rory who planned to kill her. Her tears had stopped. No, she thought, no.

"I can't believe it," she said.

"I had a hard time myself. All that lovely money. Your father must have been in the rackets, whoever he was. Dear Aunt Marie would never condone criminal money."

"What — what are you going to do?"

"You must remember you're still officially dead."

"No. Beatrice knows, Jim Halloway knows . . ."

"But I have your death certificate dated a year ago, and the bank in San Francisco where the money is certainly doesn't know you didn't die in Mexico."

"Why didn't you just let me be?" she cried. "Why didn't you take the money a year ago and forget me?"

"Because I knew you weren't dead. Where were you? Hiding, waiting to see what I'd do? Did you suspect the brakes had been tampered with, know the Ferrari crashed on purpose? How could I realize you had amnesia for the whole damn time, didn't even remember the accident?"

"I might never have remembered . . ."

"A month ago I read an ad in the *Union* about

this entertainer called Topaz at The Copper King. I had a feeling, just a feeling. I'd looked all over for you — Mexico, San Diego, even up around Porterville, around here. I was beginning to tell myself it might be safe to pretend to find that bank account of yours. After all, the will had been probated. Wherever you were you weren't watching me, I made sure of that. But then I saw the ad and went to The Copper King."

"You — you met Gill, gave him money . . ."

"That was stupid, I was rattled, not understanding yet you thought you were someone else. But you remembered all right, you knew me fast enough."

Rory was leaning against the side of the car, holding her in front of him. The sky was red and orange with the last rays of the dying sun. The ruined house was ahead of her. Where could I hide if I got away, she wondered. The windows are broken, the door is askew. I could scream but who would hear?

"Rory," she said helplessly, "I'll give you the money. I don't want it, it's not real to me."

He laughed.

Risa rammed her head back and upward as hard as she could. She felt the crack as her skull connected with Rory's jaw and his hand slackened and she broke away, running, trying to get the house between her and Rory. Run, hurry across the field, hide, there must be a place to hide, soon the dark would come and he couldn't find her in the dark.

She skirted the house, but as she swerved around the corner, her foot hit an adobe clod and she tripped, twisting her leg and sprawling headlong. I lost my chance, he'll catch up, she thought in despair, when the opening to the space under the house caught her eye. Quickly she slid sideways, pulled herself into the crawl space, rose on her hands and knees and crept into the deeper shadows. She curled on her side in the darkness, her injured leg throbbing. There was no more than three feet between the ground and the floor of the house.

Rattlesnakes, her mind said. Scorpions. Black widows. But the danger outside was worse. She forced herself to be still. I'm safe, he can't find me. There was silence. Would he give up? Leave? She strained her ears to listen for the engine. Was that a car door slamming? Yes. Now she distinctly heard the engine. The sound grew fainter, was gone.

Would he give up so easily? Rory never gave up. But I heard the car leave, she assured herself. Nevertheless, she lay motionless for some time before she cautiously got to her hands and knees and crept toward the opening to the outside. She listened. Silence. The shadows had lengthened, it was dusk.

He's gone. No, no, there's danger out there, I can't go out. She felt in her pocket for the topaz brooch, closed her hand around it. My amulet, she told herself. But what good is the topaz against a man who plans to kill me? I did hear the car start, go away. He can't be waiting for me.

She moved as quietly as she could, edging out into the twilight. She stood up, trying not to put too much weight on her left leg, which still hurt. An arm came from behind her, caught her neck in the angle of the elbow.

"Running did you no good, nor hiding in your hole. You've always been a little rabbit, afraid of everything. Don't you know rabbits never win?" Rory.

His arm tightened until she had trouble breathing.

"Walk," he said. "We'll go inside the house . . ." His words trailed off as lights flashed near the entrance to the drive.

Let it be a car, she prayed. Someone coming.

But the lights faded and no sound of a car came to them. Rory began to push her along and she realized his car was gone from the front of the house. He had driven it up the road to fool her. He'd walked back and waited . . .

"We'll go into the house," Rory said, "you love your dear old homestead, why fight against going inside?"

She was choking, she couldn't breathe, she sagged against Rory and the pressure on her throat eased.

"No," he said. "I'm not going to carry you. You walk in there on your own two feet."

Around the house, up the stairs . . .

"There won't be enough of you to identify this time," he said. "A fire in this old wreck will take care of that detail nicely. I planned something else for you, I hoped you'd come back here on your own for old times' sake and stumble into what I fixed for you nearly a year ago when I came up here to search for you. And you came, finally, almost fell into my little surprise but you were lucky again, someone pulled you out."

Risa moaned in horror and pain.

"Your run of luck is over, mine is beginning," he said. "What's the nursery rhyme? 'Will you step into my parlor . . . ?' Only it's your parlor. And we'll light a nice warm fire . . ."

"Let her go," a voice said.

Jim's name burst in Risa's mind like a beacon of light. She tried to call out to him but Rory tightened his hold, jerked both of them around to face Jim. Risa could barely see him in the gathering darkness.

"I've got a gun, in case you can't see it," Rory said. "I suppose you're the doctor, but you're too late. Or maybe just in time to join her."

❧ *19* ❧

"Let her go," Jim repeated.

Risa heard his words through the roaring in her ears. I've got to do something, she told herself. Rory is crazy, he won't listen. He'll shoot Jim.

"You can't kill us both, they're bound to find out. Think about it, Rory." Jim's voice had an edge she had never heard before.

"First you, then her," Rory said. "Who's to stop me?"

Risa began moving her hand slowly, while Rory spoke, toward her jacket pocket.

"You can both burn together in here, company for each other."

She had her hand in her pocket, had the topaz brooch in her fingers. Careful now, unfasten the safety catch, unhook the pin, you can do it with one hand, don't hurry, there, now . . .

"Stop squirming," Rory told her. "Okay, doctor, climb the steps, I can see your outline, don't try anything . . ."

Risa inched her hand up her body, up, up . . .

"Now, doctor, stop in the door there, that's right."

Risa felt the tensing of Rory's muscles. He's going to shoot, she thought, and she shoved her arm out, brought it back as hard as she could, driving the pin of the brooch into Rory's arm once, twice.

His grasp slackened and she slipped out from under his arm, the gun went off, a yellow flash in the dimness, a sharp crack. There was a thud as the two men grappled together, slipped and fell down the steps in their struggle.

Risa still had the topaz in her hand. Putting it once again in her pocket, she felt over the rough wood of the porch. She had heard the gun drop, heard it hit the porch. Had the gun bounced off onto the ground? Then her fingers touched warm metal and the gun was in her hands.

She came down the steps, circled the fighting men. Had Rory's shot hit Jim? In the dusk there was no way to tell one man from the other. After a few minutes, one of the figures arose. She backed away.

"Jim?" she asked.

There was no answer.

Not Jim? "I've got the gun," she said.

"But you won't use it on me." Rory's voice. "You can't shoot me and you know it."

Risa glanced at the unmoving figure on the ground. Had Rory killed Jim? Had he been shot after all? She backed farther away, realized with horror Rory was coming toward her. She raised the gun, tried to pull the trigger and knew Rory was right — she couldn't shoot him.

Risa turned and ran, heading across the field toward the sycamore grove. She no longer had any plan, just ran terrified, the gun useless in her hand, heading for the sanctuary she had known as a child.

She stumbled on unseen rocks, clods of adobe, but recovered and kept going. Was he behind her? In her terror and flight the wind seemed to rush by her ears so she could hear nothing else.

The sycamores were ahead of her, close now, the ghostly trunks white in the darkness, the boulders looming black between them. Risa ran on inside the grove, swerving behind the first of the boulders, where she stopped to rest. Her breath came in sobbing gasps, her chest hurt.

Was Rory there on the other side of the rock? As her breathing calmed, she leaned against the boulder and listened. Gradually the night sounds came to her, frogs piping, the querulous call of a roosting bird disturbed by her passage. Was there no pursuit? Where was Rory? Cautiously she edged around the rock, peered into the night toward the ranch house.

She saw lights, twin round circles, and it was a few minutes before she realized they were car headlights, coming nearer, coming toward the sycamore trees and the boulders where she hid. She darted in back of the rock again, moved to a place she remembered where a group of smaller rocks made a step — the pile which she had used as a child to climb up between two large rocks, where now through a crevice between the boulders she watched the car approach.

I used to play king-of-the-hill here, she thought. All by myself so I couldn't lose. The battles were against imaginary enemies. I never visualized having a real enemy, someone who wanted to kill me in order to assert his right to be king-of-the-hill.

The lights came closer, closer until the motor stopped and they lit the grove harshly. Risa heard a door slam. There was no doubt in her mind who had come, who was stalking her, would go on forever until she died. The thought of Jim brushed her consciousness but slipped away. No use. There was no way to avoid her fate, she might as well walk out into the light and hand him the gun.

She had shoved the gun into her jacket pocket to climb on the boulders and now she reached for it, felt the sharp stab of the unfastened pin of the brooch. She took the topaz in her hands and once again felt its warmth, saw the gem glow yellow-brown. Something seemed to flow into her from the topaz and she straightened, pinned the brooch over her heart. An amulet, she thought.

Risa pulled the gun from her pocket and held it ready to use. You can be the hunter, she assured herself. Wait. The frogs began to sound again and she listened to their cadence, hoping to trace Rory's movements by their stopping and starting.

A movement there, a shadow between the trees, a man, hold the gun steady, he'll walk in front of these rocks, he's coming now — Shoot. She pulled the trigger and felt the gun jerk in her hand, heard the crack. The figure disappeared. Had she hit him? Was he dead?

Risa could not decide whether to move from her concealment. Thoughts fluttered in her head. Did I miss him? Will he come and find me now? I must climb down, hide somewhere else. Is he lying dead? Hurt? Should I go see? Maybe I'll find him and he'll be bleeding, the stickiness will cover my hands and I — No, no, don't bring back Kitty's ghost.

Finally she slid the gun into her pocket and felt her way back down to the ground, quietly edged around the boulders, stopped and listened. I have to find out, she said to herself. I have to know.

The frog sounds had stopped again. From her movements? Or was Rory stalking her again, creeping as silently as she? Not lying dead at all?

She couldn't go into the glare from the car headlights where she would be seen. Follow the shadows, make no noise. Rory's killed Jim, she thought in despair. If Jim was alive he would come to the grove, come and help me. But there was no help and Rory would kill her. I can't see him, Rory's not here on the ground where he would be if my shot had hit him. I missed. She drooped in despair.

A dark form swooped low over her head, rose and flew into the night. Risa caught back her startled cry. Only an owl, a hunting owl, not the man who hunted her. Something else grabbed at her arm and she did make a slight noise of fright before she knew her jacket sleeve had snagged on a small sycamore twig. She freed herself and scurried away.

I'm like the rabbit he said I was, she chided herself. I shouldn't have left the boulders, up there was relatively safe. Instead I fled like a frightened rabbit when I could have stayed and outwaited him. I have the gun, he couldn't have reached me up there except by climbing. I would have had the chance to shoot him as he climbed.

Now it was too late to go back. Rory might be anywhere between her and the rocks, might even be waiting there, watching her now from her own former vantage point.

He can't see me, she reassured herself, but in vain. Eyes were on her, as before at The Copper King an unseen pursuer followed each movement. But now she moved toward a rendezvous.

Risa felt almost as though she were sleepwalking among the sycamores as she used to when a child. Sleepwalking, between the boulders, between the dream world and the real. Soon she would wake, must wake and find . . . But she was already awake, no longer could she lose herself in the labyrinths of her own mind. She was no longer able to escape being Risa MacArthur who had also been Kitty Morgan.

Had her mother come here at night, frightened, to pry a board loose and hide the Mason jar? Why? Because her mother knew her sister Marie too well, knew she would destroy the letters, Tony's and their grandmother's? Did my mother have a premonition of her death and really come here to tell me of the present of the topaz, whisper the words to me that I remembered somehow, small as I was?

Risa shook her head. And yet there had been the dreams of her childhood, the sleepwalking, always to this grove. In search of what?

Her left leg hurt so much she had difficulty walking. The ache filled her mind until she grew dizzy. She slumped in the deep shadow of a boulder where two trees joined at the ground to form a massive single trunk. She fought against the spinning, the concentric circles dragging her downward into unconsciousness. Rory was searching for her in the darkness and she must stay alert. Even now she could scarcely believe Rory wanted to kill her.

He had come into The Copper King when she played the piano, played and sang and was Topaz without any past. What had he thought of Topaz? But he hadn't even noticed, all he saw was the person who stood between him and the money.

If he killed her he would have the topaz brooch too, perhaps give it to Allegra, he wouldn't need to sell it. Risa straightened, unable to bear the thought of Allegra wearing her topaz. No, no, Rory must never get the topaz brooch.

The night now seemed unnaturally quiet. She could feel the pulsing of blood in her head, almost hear the pounding. Was Rory hiding too, waiting for her to make a betraying movement, a revealing sound? If he was close enough, could he hear the rush of her breath in and out?

Fingers trembling, she unpinned the topaz from her jacket and slipped out of her crevice, limping but moving with quiet purpose. If she dropped the topaz into the old well Rory would not find it. She paused, momentarily frozen by the hideous realization Rory was the person who had found the old hay fork and thrown it into the well on his trip up to the ranch when he was still searching for her. What had he said? That this wasn't his first surprise? He had set the trap hoping she would fall in and kill herself — a very faint possibility since he didn't even know where she was at the time. Could anyone leave a trap set like that, not caring that somebody else might stumble into it and die? Not even Rory . . .

But Risa could see him prying up the boards, knocking out the rotten posts, exposing the well. She had prattled on about the old well often enough to him, telling him of her hideaway in the sycamore grove and her adventures there. Now in the darkness she pictured Rory dropping the broken hay fork into the hole and turning his back, walking away, not caring that a total stranger might lose his life, thinking only that Risa might die if she ever came back to the ranch. Not selling the ranch, saving it for her so she could die in another arranged accident.

As she had almost done, would have done except for Jim. If Jim was dead what difference did it make to die herself? Except Rory must not have the topaz. Allegra must never wear the brooch over her heart.

Risa came to the well by a circuitous route, approaching from the far side of the grove. He can't see me before I drop the topaz in the hole, she thought. He must never know. The gun too. I'll throw the gun in and then he can't take it from me.

But as she neared the opening she had to step into a clearing, away from the friendly shadows. The headlight beams did not penetrate well this far away but their diffused light made contrasts that would show a moving figure. She approached cautiously, stepped out of the concealing darkness with dread.

Risa could not see the well opening but knew where it must be because of the familiar landmarks, the dead tree there, fallen across two of its living neighbors, the oddly shaped rock . . .

There was a triumphant shout and a sudden rush of movement in front of her. Risa stood transfixed, then cried out. Rory. Would he reach her before she could — But no, he was headed wrong, he was going to . . .

There was a crash, a scream that rang in her ears even after the sound of falling faded away.

❧ 20 ❧

The well, the open well — he had been on the other side of it when he started after her. Had he fallen in? But what had made the crash, the sound of metal on metal? She was afraid to get too near the hole, afraid now of falling herself.

She backed away, skirted around the area in a wide semicircle and hurried as fast as she could with her injured leg toward the headlights of the car. Rory's gold Jaguar stood at the edge of the grove with the lights on but he had taken the key. She stumbled across the field toward the ranch house and Jim. Was Jim . . . ?

A dark figure loomed in her path and she stopped, unable to make a sound.

Rory, she thought. He's not in the well, I can't escape, I'll never escape him.

"Risa?"

Was it — could it be Jim's voice?

A light flicked in her face, went off. "Are you all right?"

"Oh, Jim, Jim, I was afraid he'd shot you, that you were dead."

He held her against him and she reached her hands up to his head, felt wetness under her fingers.

"You *are* hurt. You're bleeding."

"He hit me with a rock," Jim said. "I'm okay

211

now, knocked me out for a while. Where is he? Do you have the gun?"

"I think he's in the well, he is, yes, he is, he fell." Risa was aware she was babbling, couldn't seem to stop. "I tried to shoot but I couldn't, then I did but he didn't die, he's in the well . . ."

Jim held her close, bent and kissed her mouth so she couldn't speak, and after a moment she relaxed, clung to him.

"We'll go look," Jim said. "Give me the gun." He turned on his flashlight.

They did not see Rory at first under the twisted metal at the bottom of the well, then Risa saw the copper hair gleam in the circle of light and turned away.

"The hay fork," Jim said. "But we hauled it out, the man was supposed to come back and . . ."

"I — I heard Rory stumble," Risa said. "He saw me and started to run. The hay fork must have been there, right by the well opening like it was left, Rory couldn't see it and fell onto it, then he and the fork went into the well. Is he — do you think . . . ?"

"He'd need a miracle to survive." Jim's voice was grim. "There's no way we can get him out without help, so even if he's not dead yet . . ." His voice trailed off.

They walked across the field, up the drive to Jim's car, parked near the access road, taking a long time because Risa could hardly walk.

"I won't wait here," she cried when Jim had

proposed getting his car and driving across the field to pick her up. "I'll crawl first."

"I left the car there," he explained, pointing, "because the gold sports car I'd seen before was parked at *this* spot. When I saw it I knew I'd guessed right, the only two places you would be were here or Baja. I got out and walked to the house and you know what happened then. I couldn't actually believe he was going to kill you — I hadn't expected a gun."

"How did you find me, decide to come to the ranch?"

"I came out of the hospital in time to see you get into a gold sports car and I knew it was the car I'd seen in Baja. I waited awhile and then went out to Del Mar, expecting you'd be there. By then I was almost sure the mystery man had to be Rory. Neither of you were there but Allegra was, and we had a heart-to-heart session. She admitted Rory knew you were alive, had from the first day you came home, admitted he drove a gold sports car. When you didn't show up I got scared. She was too, though she didn't admit it. But she told me to go to the ranch, she had a feeling he had headed here. I knew it was here or Baja and I decided to believe her."

"You suspected Rory? I never did, not at all, not until the last . . ."

"Long ago. I still don't know why he turned killer, but when you told me he'd buried a girl he thought was you I couldn't buy that. Or this strange disappearance of his after you remembered you were Risa and went home."

"Why didn't you tell me what you suspected?"

"You loved him, you wouldn't have listened to me."

"No, not love. Worship maybe, like a child. Hero worship. But you're right, I wouldn't have believed you." I hardly believe it now, Risa thought. Rory, the bright handsome god of her childhood had tried to kill her. And now he was dead.

Jim put her into the car. As he walked around to get in himself, she looked back across the field and saw the lights of the Jaguar, shining the way to Rory's grave. She shuddered.

Jim got in and started the motor. "I'll have to call the police."

"The sheriff," she said. She was trembling all over, her teeth chattering.

"I'm going to stop at a motel first," he said. "You've got to lie down or you'll collapse." He reached over and took her hand. "It's reaction," he said. "You'll be all right but you need to rest. I'm not going to drag you through anything more."

When he helped her into the motel room, Risa stared at his blood-smeared face, the laceration on the side of his head, where dark encrusted blood matted the hair. "I'm surprised they rented you a room," she said. "You look awful."

Jim grimaced. "I've felt better. I told them we'd been in an accident," he said. "They were very helpful, even called the sheriff's office for me. I'm to wait here for the deputy."

Risa was sitting on the edge of the bed and he pressed her gently back onto the pillows. "Your face is almost as white as that pillowcase," he said, sitting beside her. "Try to relax. I'll be back as soon as I can."

She reached for his arm, grasped it tightly. "Don't go away," she said. "I can't bear to . . ."

He stroked her head, ran his hand along her cheek. "Everything will be all right," he repeated.

"You don't — don't even know why he — why Rory wanted to kill me," she said.

"You're safe, he didn't succeed, he'll never trouble you again." He unclasped her fingers from his arm and held her hand. "But I can guess. You made a will out to him so there must have been money you didn't know about but he did."

"From my father," she said.

"Have you remembered everything, your lost year, all that happened?"

"Yes. I even remember not knowing you in the hospital when you called me Risa and I — I — Oh, Jim, how could I have done that?"

"It doesn't matter now."

She looked into the hazel eyes, saw the glints of gold. With her free hand she fumbled the topaz out of her pocket, clutched it in her palm. Then she opened her hand to show what she held. "This is the topaz brooch. Do you remember?"

For the first time a smile touched his mouth.

He ran his fingers along her face. Then he took the topaz from her and examined it. "A lovely piece of antique jewelry," he said. He held the brooch just above her palm. The smile had spread to his eyes.

"For Risa," he said:

> *"A topaz for my Lady Fair,*
> *November born so she may wear*
> *The golden sun within this stone,*
> *An amulet for her alone*
> *To keep her safe from violent harm*
> *And bring her love and gentle charm."*

He dropped the topaz into her hand, closed his own hand around hers. "A gift of love," he said. "The first of many."